Praise for *Trevelyan's Wager*

"Trevelyan's Wager made me think . . . will we truly be happy if we live forever?"

—*Penny For My Thoughts*

Trevelyan's Wager

by
David Bassano

Harvard Square Editions
New York
2016

Published in the United States by
Harvard Square Editions
www.HarvardSquareEditions.org

ISBN: 978-1-941861-19-6

Printed in the United States of America

Author's Introduction to the First Edition

It has been three years since I signed my first contract with McClellan Publishers. At the time, I had just received the Pulitzer-MacArthur Award for my book on the Global Solidarity Alliance and its movement to support 'alternative states' around the world. Based on the success of that book, McClellan advanced me a considerable sum to write a compendium of rebellions around the world, to be published under their 'Current Affairs' imprint.

This is not the book I was paid to write. There may be some at McClellan who are upset by the change of plans, but I wrote this book because I had to. At first, I thought my invitation to Elysium would take my career to new and unknown heights, but the project went from professional to personal very quickly. In retrospect, I wonder whether my initial interest was truly professional. Perhaps it was, given how ambitious I was, or maybe ambition was only an excuse to justify another desire I had. I no longer need to justify it to myself or anyone else. I wrote what I had to write, and now I'm going to act on what I learned from writing it, although I don't yet know how I'll do that or what the consequences will be, because it's better than continuing with a lost cause. You can call that del Grappa's Wager.

And I wouldn't have published this book if I thought the questions and problems in it are mine alone. I suspect I am not alone.

William del Grappa
Paris, France
May, 2177

Chapter 1

IN MARCH OF '75, I was in Ville de Quebec, conducting research on the FDG in Northern Labrador for the new McClellan book. I planned to travel north after the spring thaw for interviews and photographs. I had already been in Quebec for two months in the depths of its winter, the gloom interrupted only by the lively winter carnival. Even carnival is not very amusing when you're alone, and I had been alone for months, researching and traveling, and my only conversations had been with taxi drivers, waiters, and the occasional girl in a café. Since I was in Quebec I decided, after some deliberation, to give Rallie a call.

I had been introduced to Rallie in New York at a dinner party hosted by a literary agent. He was a socialite whose source of income seemed vague and variable. His interest in me increased after someone mentioned my recent Pulitzer-MacArthur. He was friendly enough though I found that he talked too much. I wouldn't have called him that day in Quebec if I hadn't been so tired of being alone with books. I hoped the evening would go differently than I expected, and it did.

Rallie said he was happy to hear from me and wanted to know where I'd been and who I'd met. Then he told me there was an art gallery opening in the Old City that evening. He invited me to join him there, assuring me there would be excellent food and wine as well as some very unusual people. I asked him if there would also be some good art and he said he thought there probably would be. I told him I'd like to attend, but did not have very good clothes with me since I'd been traveling for the purpose of research. He ordered me to Louis LaFlamme on rue St. Jean to find something. I told him my budget would not permit it. He then tried to think of any of his associates in Quebec who might be approximately my size and willing to lend me an outfit for the evening. I suggested that my title of freelance writer would excuse my wardrobe, and he reluctantly agreed it probably would.

I took a cab to the gallery, stopping along the way at a bar for a bourbon while the cab waited out front. Rallie met me at the gallery, immaculately dressed. He examined the paintings quickly so he could comment on them. Then he introduced me to the various artists, critics, dealers, and patrons in the room. I was impressed by his memory of not just names and faces but of complete biographies and the relationships between everyone. I wondered what he had to say about me when I wasn't there. I was thinking about how I might get away from him to eavesdrop when I spotted a young woman across the room.

She was about five and a half feet tall with long, thick, dark brown hair, and I guessed she was twenty or twenty-one. She wore a simple black satin dress with a threadlike choker and small diamond earrings. I stood watching her with champagne in my hand as people were brought to her for an introduction. It was as if she was discreetly holding court. Behind her were four large men who could only have been bodyguards. She was very beautiful and, although I couldn't hear the conversations, I could see her almost preternatural confidence and commanding presence. But I had an odd feeling as I watched her closely. She was too beautiful – she was *impossibly* beautiful.

One of the bodyguards nodded to Rallie, who excused himself from his conversation, took me by the arm, and led me to the young woman.

"Miss Sophia Trevelyan," he said, "may I introduce Mr. William del Grappa."

"Pleased to meet you," I said.

She had a firm handshake and unwavering eye contact.

"*Our Future and Theirs*," she said.

"Yes, that was mine."

"Outstanding work," she said. "Congratulations on the Pulitzer-MacArthur."

"Thank you." I noticed she wore no makeup at all.

"Miss Trevelyan just won the competition to design the new wing of the Louvre," said Rallie.

"You're an architect?" I asked.

"Of sorts," she said. "I take projects here and there when something appealing comes along. I did the Kolowski Museum in Warsaw."

"If you don't mind my asking," I said, "how old are you?" Even I knew that was uncouth, but I had to do it.

She smiled playfully, a little girl's smile, bright-eyed, like she knew a secret. Her eyes were amazing – blue, black, brown, green, and gold, like a mosaic of glass shards.

Rallie stepped closer and lowered his voice.

"Miss Trevelyan is from Elysium."

"No kidding?"

"No kidding," she said.

"I've never met anyone from Elysium," I said.

"I've never met a war correspondent," she said. "No doubt it's much more interesting than living on Elysium."

"It's got its moments."

"From your book, I should say so. What are you working on these days?"

"A compendium of all the world's insurgencies, with analyses and interviews."

"Do you think you'll be under fire again?" she asked.

I felt the familiar murmur in the back of my mind.

"Almost certainly," I said.

"Take me with you?" she said with her nymphish grin.

I laughed.

"I thought she'd find your work appealing," said Rallie, beaming.

"You'd really like to see combat?" I asked.

"Yes and no," she said. "I'm sure you know what I mean."

"I do know."

"I promise I wouldn't get in the way…"

"I'll swap ya," I said.

"For?"

"Take me to Elysium."

Rallie chuckled, but his smile faded when he realized I wasn't joking.

"No one's ever reported on a visit there," I said to Sophia. "Let me interview you on Elysium. And I'll take you with me on my next assignment."

She looked at the floor, thinking.

Rallie shifted nervously. "Well, I'm sure that's a bit much to ask, William."

"Give me your card," she said. "It's something to consider."

I gave her my card and we talked briefly about the show in the gallery before Rallie led me away to make room for the next courtier.

Rallie continued to work the room for the next two hours while I perused the artwork, trying to hear what it was trying to say. I couldn't access any of it. Then from across the room I saw Rallie look at his watch. I walked over to him.

"Let's go for a drink," I said.

"We might as well," he said. "The gallery will be open for another hour, but nothing is going to happen."

"Where's Sophia?"

"I don't know. She probably went home. They never stay out of the annexes for long."

"Where's the nearest annex?"

"Montreal."

We took a cab to the lower town to an ancient café called *Anges et Diables*. Rallie looked tired.

"You really blew it tonight," he said.

"Ya think so?"

"Ask for something no one's ever been given, in the first few seconds of knowing her?"

"She asked for quite a bit herself."

"That's her place," he said, "not yours."

"I've never known my place."

"I know. I'm trying to show you how useful it is to understand these things. Doors would open for you."

I open my own doors, buddy, I thought.

I knew I had no right to judge Rallie. I used people, too. Writers usually do, especially those of us who conduct interviews as part of our work. People let me into their secret worlds of rebellion and insurgency, of tightly-knit communities suspicious of outsiders. They always used me for something – publicity or fame or the chance to get their voice into the historical record. In return I got material for articles and books. I came into their conflicts, their lives and communities, lived with them, recorded the stories and took the photos, then got out before the odds caught up with me, leaving them to face the dangers while I went back. Back to Amsterdam or Paris where I could get high and laid and enjoy all the benefits of civilization. Then eventually I'd get bored with that, with the safety, predictability, and convenience, and make arrangements to go back. Back to the world of life and death, of things that really mattered and how alive it made me feel, and the people there and the unspoken agreement into which we'd entered. So I was really no better than Rallie in the end.

"How old is she?" I asked.

"I don't know," he said. "Older than us, that's for sure."

"It would be incredible if I got that interview."

"It's not gonna happen. You have to cultivate this kind of relationship carefully. Especially with a woman of her station. It's not like cutting a deal with a guerilla in Latin America."

"If she forgets me, I haven't lost anything," I said.

"*I* have," he said. "It's not easy to stay in the scene. You have to make people feel comfortable and safe around you. That's how you get invited back, get invited *in*. That's how you make connections and gain advantages. But if you're too brazen, you'll be ignored."

"Or *you* get ignored."

"Exactly. Now if she thinks I'm going to bring people around who are too forward, I won't be able to get anywhere near her. And then she'll tell other people, too."

"If I caused you trouble tonight," I said, "I apologize."

He sighed. "Try to be more careful from now on, please. This is delicate business. It will help your career, but it must be done carefully."

So Rallie's efforts to use me to use Sophia, for whatever purpose he had, hadn't worked. Or at least he didn't think so. But I knew how Sophia felt. She might change her mind about seeing the other side of the world, or she might panic and run at the first sign of trouble, as even journalists sometimes did. If she'd really been bitten by the bug, though, it might be enough to get me invited to Elysium, in which case I would have surpassed Rallie at his own game.

I swallowed the rest of my scotch.

"Hey Rallie."

"Hmm?"

"Thank you."

"You're impossible," he said. "And you're welcome."

Chapter 2

RALLIE WOULD HAVE BEEN SHOCKED to hear that Sophia contacted me eight weeks later, and that I was the first visitor to be invited to Elysium, but I never bothered to tell him. I cancelled my research plans and flew to Marseille. From there I would take a private aircraft to the island. These flights were used to ferry supplies to Elysium, as well as facilitate the occasional trip to the 'outside,' such as the one Sophia had made to Quebec. At a small airport by the coast, I was subjected to intense questioning by Elysium security personnel, although they had already conducted background checks. They drew a blood sample, then conducted retina scans and minutely searched my luggage. The last two procedures required most of the three hours it took to complete the blood analysis. They told me I had been exposed to dangerous pathogens in the past, but that none were currently active in my system. I asked for the names of the offending pathogens and they refused to tell me. What I needed to know was that I was cleared to travel to Elysium. Then came a legal harangue about how my visit was a privilege, not a right, and that Elysium was private property, and I was subject to expulsion without warning, explanation, or appeal. I signed several statements indemnifying the Elysium Corporation of anything that happened to me during the visit, and was again questioned about my purposes, and whether or not I had any weapons, outside food, or chemical agents. No, I do not have a pet in my carry-on luggage. No, the only electronic item I am carrying is the audio recording device I have already declared. No, I am not trained in the martial arts. Finally, they put me on the aircraft for the short flight.

I am not going to say much about the science of genetic engineering, or the breakthrough which finally allowed *Homo sapiens* to arrest the aging process. At this time, the exact process remains a closely-guarded secret of the Elysium Corporation, and there has been a great deal of speculation by people far more knowledgeable on the subject than I am. But the history of Elysium is fairly straightforward, and certainly worth relating.

In the 2020s, genetic engineering had advanced to the point where pre-fertilization manipulation of DNA, by various methods, could produce a host of outcomes in the human body. Some were cosmetic, such as predetermining the sex, eye and hair color, and so on in the child. Other advances were more significant, such as complete resistance to diseases such as cancer or dementia. The processes were expensive, and few could afford to have them performed on the mother's egg before having it implanted. There were several companies carrying out these procedures, but the Elysium Corporation was foremost among them.

In 2059 the Elysium Corporation announced, to widespread skepticism, that it had achieved the holy grail of genetic engineering: arresting the aging process. Human cells could be programmed to age until a certain point, and then simply regenerate themselves without the subsequent deterioration we call physical aging. Several organizations had been experimenting with genetically-modified telomeres, the deterioration of which causes cells to stop replicating properly. The Elysium Corporation was the only one to succeed. Some experts conjectured that

Elysium had spliced cancer cell DNA into human ones, since cancer cells restore their telomeres and are thus theoretically immortal. Others speculated that simple splicing wasn't enough, and that the task required a complete rebuild of the DNA ladder through molecular engineering. The question remains unanswered, since the corporation has never revealed its method.

Elysium's only cooperation with the scientific community was to have DNA tests conducted on children born with the modification. Experts could then verify that the process worked, by observing that a modified individual showed no physical signs of aging, even at the cellular level. The corporation needed this verification for legal purposes. Someone claiming to be a thousand years old would arouse suspicion if their identity was challenged.

The announcement in 2059 was published worldwide, but the corporation made no further comment. No press releases, no interviews, not even answers for journalists. As a result, no one really believed it was true until the United Nations scientific team verified the claim in 2100, when the first 'immortal' individual was forty-one years old and had the body of a twenty-one year-old. Death had officially been conquered — the greatest technological advance in history. And the Elysium Corporation didn't release a single statement.

Not that the rest of the world wasn't talking. There had been protests since the first significant advances in human GM (Genetic Modification), when certain inherited diseases were eliminated and hooked noses straightened before birth. There was an even more aggressive reaction after the UN confirmation of Elysium's success with GM-IM (Genetic Modification — Immortal). Religious leaders rejected GM as a perversion of God's plan. Humanists claimed it was weakening the gene pool through unnatural selection. Socialists pointed to the injustice of the wealthy living longer, or in this case, perhaps forever. It was particularly ironic that GM-IM was achieved as humanity was suffering the consequences of global warming. Sea levels rose and hurricanes became more frequent; while coastal areas had too much water, regions farther inland had far too little. About half a billion people were on the move at any time, seeking dry land or fresh water. Tropical diseases spread into formerly temperate areas, and farmers without the credit to buy genetically-modified, heat-resistant crops went bankrupt. Global capital had concentrated wealth into an ever-smaller group, so that while a handful of people could afford genetic modifications, half the world could barely afford to eat. All this fueled the social instability from which I'd been making my living as a journalist.

The Elysium Corporation quickly became one of the most profitable companies in the world, a particularly impressive accomplishment considering the small number of clients able to afford the procedure. Immortality for one's children was the greatest luxury, the greatest gift one could give. What good were estates, companies, yachts, and an Oxford degree, if you were only going to die anyway? Now that death was optional, it made more sense to spend the money on the procedure.

Legal attempts to stop Elysium were launched, but precautions were in place. Research, modification, and insemination were conducted in countries which had not outlawed human GM, or even on ships in international waters, and the impregnated women returned to their own countries to bear the child. There were scattered cases of violence against

GM children and their parents, so the corporate headquarters and research facilities were heavily guarded.

In 2050, private interests purchased the four-island archipelago called Îles d'Hyères from the cash-strapped government of France. The collapse of the global economy from climate change had ruined the tourist trade that supported the small population of the islands. Many of their homes were partially submerged by rising sea levels. The purchasing conglomerate owned the islands for only six years before selling them to the Elysium Corporation at a slim profit. By that time, they had removed all signs of habitation from the islands. Some later accused Elysium of having formed the conglomerate in the first place to do its bidding.

The corporation changed the name of the largest island, Île du Levant, to Elysium, and began a long legal process by which it secured a maximum of sovereignty from France. It maintained its own security force and infrastructures, which the government could not have afforded anyway, and in return the corporation paid very low taxes to operate there. By the time GM-IM was verified, there was nothing Elysium's critics could do to move the corporation off the islands.

The corporation left the three smallest islands of the archipelago unoccupied for the time being, and invested its profits in Elysium, building infrastructure and clearing land for homes. It set up a powerful defense system and tried to make Elysium the safest place on Earth. It then sold property to the immortal children. Threats and occasional violence against GM-IM individuals (typically called IMs or, simply, 'Immortals') were enough to make them consider relocating to the island. Safety was now their primary concern. What good is it to never age, if some accident will eventually kill you? And what good to live among mortals? You'll watch them all grow old and senile and die. You're better off in the company of other Immortals, with whom you can share eternity. On Elysium you could have all that, and in great luxury. Within a few years, all the Immortals had taken the option of buying property on Elysium and emigrating there. When they had IM children of their own, the children also lived on the island. There were probably no more than two hundred IMs on the island, plus their unmodified servants and guards. The corporation's investments ensured their lifestyle could continue forever.

That was about all the outside world knew about Elysium from legal documents and a few interviews with Immortals when they visited the annexes. The corporation had no motivation to educate the public about its activities. Everyone rich enough to afford immortality already knew about it. Eventually, the Immortals themselves purchased the corporation — the original owners all being dead — and ran the island like a sovereign nation.

I watched out the window the entire flight. The Mediterranean off the Côte d'Azur was dotted with white sailboats and yachts. Then I spotted one of the corporation's ships on patrol and knew we were close. This area was completely restricted: no unauthorized aircraft or shipping allowed, and intruders were dealt with sternly.

Finally I saw a large, sunny island covered in flowering trees. There was a village and a harbor, but only a few small boats and no sign of industry. The men in the aircraft took their eyes off me for the first time during the trip to gaze out the windows as we gently banked for our landing.

Chapter 3

IT WASN'T MUCH of a welcome. I was met off the aircraft by a security detail that took me into a lovely little house that looked lifted out of Cinque Terre. Inside, they began another round of questioning, to see if my answers matched those I gave in France, I guess. It reminded me of certain encounters I'd had as a journalist, when I'd been stopped by suspicious soldiers who didn't believe my story and thought I was a spy. They were humorless and didn't want me there. I stopped taking such things personally long ago. I noticed, however, that none of them was armed, not even with a truncheon.

After an hour of questioning and waiting, they took me outside and handed me my bag. A small, open-top electric vehicle pulled up silently, and I was told it would take me to Sophia's villa. I got in and the driver took us down the road without a word. I wasn't in the mood to try to engage him.

The road led to the seaside village I'd seen from the air. It was a small community spreading up a hill behind the harbor, with colorful buildings and narrow cobblestone streets, and it looked like a picture from a child's book of fairy tales with its arched doorways, terracotta roofs, window boxes of flowers, vine-covered stucco walls, and beautifully-decorated shops. There were a dozen or so people on the broad sidewalks. The streets were clean, perfectly clean, and the buildings looked well-kept — no peeling paint, no bowed rooflines. Iron streetlamps lined the sidewalks. In the town center was marble fountain, inlaid with what looked like gold, surrounded by gardens and an open square. The air was clean and crisp, and smelled of the sea and, I thought, flowers. There were only two other vehicles on the road; being electric, they made almost no sound. The town was very quiet, and sound of the fountain carried a long way.

The driver wordlessly took us up the hill behind the town on a winding road through an evergreen forest. It was cooler up here, and the light was beautiful through the pines with the scent of the trees. We reached a plateau and came to an estate; the road was lined with poplars, and beyond them were orchards on either side. Then came a wide lawn, and the road made a cul-de-sac in front of a villa. There was no security, or at least none visible. The driver stopped in front of the door, which was flanked by marble statues of nymphs. Two menservants were waiting there and met the car the moment it stopped, opening the door for me.

"Welcome to Hesperides, Mr. del Grappa, residence of Miss Sophia Trevelyan."

They carried my bag and led me through the front door to the parlor. It was a semicircular room with a high ceiling and broad windows and skylights, and a balcony looked down from the second floor. The exposed ceiling beams were tree branches, and the room was lined with small orange trees in terracotta pots. The furniture was graceful wrought iron and white pine, and there were bookshelves against the back wall. Between the bookshelves were bas reliefs of scenes from Greek mythology. The room was breezy and the leaves of the orange trees danced. The bookshelves and carvings were partially hidden from the entrance, so the room drew you in as you tried to satisfy your curiosity.

Sophia rose from a loveseat. She was dressed in English riding clothes, with leather boots and a light seersucker jacket. She wore her hair down with only tiny diamond studs in her ears. I found her more attractive now than in Quebec, if that was possible.

"Mr. del Grappa," she said, shaking my hand, "Very good to see you again."

"Likewise, Miss Trevelyan."

"Welcome to Elysium."

"Thank you. I've never seen a place so beautiful."

"And you have seen a lot of the world."

"Quite a bit of it." But I didn't usually stay in the beautiful places.

I sat across a coffee table from her, and a servant brought me tea in a beautiful china cup. Sophia asked what I had been doing and how my trip had been. I didn't have any adventures to report. Since she was dressed for riding, I asked if she had been out earlier.

"No, but I thought you might enjoy a ride around the grounds," she said, "unless you're tired from your trip."

"No, I'd love to look around."

After I finished my tea, she took me to the back deck, where servants held the reigns of two magnificent thoroughbreds. I hadn't ridden in a while, not since Pakistan, but I thought it would be a pleasant way to see the estate, even though I knew I'd be sore afterwards. We mounted and Sophia led us at a trot straight across the lawn to a line of poplars, and beyond that to an arched gate in a stone wall and up a hill.

The countryside, for beauty, was second to none. The hills were sometimes steep, but the views were breathtaking and the breeze was cool. The south of France was dry this time of year, but the vegetation here was lush, and the streams we forded were running high, cascading down the hillsides in falls. The aromatic grasses and trees we passed constantly changed the scent in the air as we rode. I came alongside Sophia.

"Is this all your land?"

"We are on the outer edge of it now," she said. "But it's an unwritten rule that people here don't fence off their properties. No one minds if you drift onto their land."

I wanted to start asking many questions, but didn't have my recorder with me; anyway, I was more interested in the scenery at the time.

She took us down into a narrow valley filled with very old trees and a rocky stream. Mist clung to the upper branches of the canopy. It looked like we were the first people to ever come through. The riding was somewhat difficult, but the horses took it perfectly, and Sophia looked completely natural in the saddle.

"You're very quiet," she said.

"I wouldn't want to ruin it."

She smiled.

At the end of the valley, we went up a small grassy hill to the ruin of a stone farmhouse with pink clematis covering the remaining walls. Sophia's menservants, in outfits reminiscent of cavalry uniforms, had ridden to the spot and laid out a thick blanket with covered trays and bottles along the edges.

"Hungry?" asked Sophia.

"Sure."

We dismounted and sat on the blanket while the servants wordlessly took our horses and served us. The plates were sturdy but beautiful china, but what surprised me was the lack of cutlery. I was given a satin sleeve containing two heavy, blunt-tipped chopsticks of jade inlaid with gold, and a silver spoon.

"No weapons allowed on Elysium," said Sophia, "not even knives and forks."

She spoke quietly to the servants, giving instructions that were instantly obeyed in silence. They offered me a glass of Vouvrey, which I accepted; I think Sophia had some sort of tea. The fare they served us could have come from the top restaurants of New York. We had a cold golden tomato bisque, fingerling potatoes in white wine, and lobster and mussels in a tomato garlic vinaigrette.

The view from the hill looked down the valley we had come up, and from there out to sea for miles.

I held up my wine glass.

"Cheers," I said. "Thanks for lunch."

"Cheers. Not at all."

I took a sip and held it in my mouth for a long time.

"It's Baumard," she said.

"Outstanding."

"I guessed you'd be okay with chopsticks," she said. "How much time have you spent in Asia?"

"I'm not sure. Burma, Indonesia…. Asian Russia, which is more like China than anything else. A lot of time." It seemed odd to eat with chopsticks while drinking Vouvrey.

"How can the cooks work without knives?" I asked.

"They have food processors for that," she said.

"This is definitely the best meal I've ever eaten with chopsticks."

"Do you miss good food when you're in the field?"

"Sure. At some point or another, you miss everything. Certain foods. A warm bed. Air conditioning. Old friends to talk to. Something to distract you from where you really are."

"And yet you always go back," she said.

"There's a wildness to it you can't get in civilization. Home is comfortable. It's easy. But you can fall asleep at home. That's why people let years slip away from them there. There's no edge to it."

"That's why I want to see the world you live in."

"I know. And I'll keep my promise."

She smiled. "I've no doubt. Did you see Gambelli's review of your book?"

"No."

"He says you're the greatest war correspondent who's ever lived."

"He mighta said it, but it isn't true."

"I knew you'd say that. But I think he may be right. When I think of the things you've seen…they are things I wouldn't even have imagined until I read your work. It's like they happened in some other world."

"You sure you want to see them?" I asked.

"Most definitely. The excitement must be incredible. You're watching history happen, right before your eyes. You're right in the middle of it all."

"Usually the middle of trouble."

"That's why you do it, isn't it? I want to feel that, too. I just can't fathom the courage you must have, going into those places. Anyway, I know I'll be safe with you. Nothing is going to happen to you. It can't."

I smiled and continued eating.

You can't protect someone in the places I went. Seems I'd grown cold enough to invite this *ingénue* into a war zone, knowing I couldn't keep her safe, so that I could advance my career with her interviews. Hell, she's not a girl, even though she looks like one, I thought. She knows what she's asking for. But I looked down the valley to the sea so that I didn't have to look into those eyes.

After we finished eating, she asked, "Is there anything else you'd like to see before we go back?"

"Yes. I'd like to see these horses run."

"I can show you that," she said with a grin.

Chapter 4

Sophia's Transcripts, Part I

WDG: IT'S MAY 5TH, 2175, 1030 HOURS local time on the island of Elysium. My name is William del Grappa, and I am at the residence of Sophia Trevelyan. I am going to interview Ms. Trevelyan on a wide range of topics regarding the Immortals and life on Elysium.

I'd first like to enter it into the official transcript that I am greatly indebted to Ms. Trevelyan for this unprecedented opportunity.

Sophia Trevelyan: You're most welcome, Mr. del Grappa.

WdG: I'd like to start with the basics. Your full name, date and place of birth, and so on.

ST: My name is Sophia Lisette Trevelyan. I am the only child of Charles Trevelyan II and Rose Trevelyan. I was born in Toronto, Canada on March 12, 2065. I am one hundred and ten years old.

WdG: That makes you one of the original residents of Elysium, doesn't it?

ST: Yes. I came here when I was twelve.

WdG: I was under the impression that GM-IM children were born here.

ST: They are now. But I was born four years before people began living here. And my parents wanted me with them for the first few years of my life despite the danger.

WdG: What danger?

ST: The usual dangers. Crime, toxins, disease, accidents...

WdG: Why didn't your parents come with you to Elysium?

ST: It wasn't allowed. The only mortals allowed on Elysium are the servants. They go through intensive screening first. Actually, we prefer to bring them here as young adolescents, so that we can indoctrinate them ourselves. But once they're here, they're not allowed to leave. Or communicate with the outside world.

WdG: For security?

ST: Correct. Their pay goes to their families; that's the motivation. They're very well-paid for their jobs.

WdG: Why did your parents choose to send you at age twelve?

ST: Many children of my age were going off to boarding school at the time. My parents thought it would be good for me to start living on Elysium, because it was safer.

WdG: Where did you live when you came?

ST: At the school. My nannies were mortals.

WdG: What about your teachers?

ST: They were mortal, too. Same criteria as the servants: no leaving, no communication. They were paid enormous sums. Enough to make their families rich.

WdG: Are there still mortal teachers here?

ST: No. The IMs now take turns teaching, once the children are teenagers. The Immortals have lived long enough to know as much on different subjects as any mortal professor.

WdG: Who teaches them before they're teens?

ST: Parents. Or another IMs. There are no educational requirements here, of course. No mandatory schooling. But everyone wants their children to have a classical education.

WdG: Did you get to see your parents after you immigrated here?

ST: Twice a year, usually. I'd fly to the annex in New York and they'd come and meet me. That was before they started the Montreal annex.

WdG: What are the annexes like?

ST: Well, you know that they are corporate property outside Elysium. The purpose is so the IMs can travel off the island to visit friends or do some sightseeing, and still have a secure environment.

WdG: The servants are under the same restrictions there?

ST: All the same rules apply. No weapons or toxins and so on.

WdG: I know there have been several attacks against them.

ST: That's true. All unsuccessful. Each annex is a self-contained fortress.

WdG: How many are there?

ST: New York, Montreal, Buenos Aires, Paris, Rome, London, Tokyo, Beijing, and Cairo. There are also several large yachts we can use as floating annexes.

WdG: Your parents would meet you at the annex?

ST: Yes. In fact, a lot of people in the corporation wanted me to meet you in one, instead of bringing you here.

WdG: How did you convince them?

ST: That's a long story.

WdG: Okay. But I can't help but notice that all the concern with safety…seems to cast some doubt on the title of Immortal.

ST: GM-IM is real, but immortality, eternal life, is just a theory. And it can never be proven.

WdG: Please explain.

ST: We do not physically age past the terminal point. For most of us, that's age twenty-one, which was chosen because it's the age at which the body is healthiest. After that, we stop aging. But that has nothing to do with other causes of death. There are also externals: disease, toxins, accidents, homicide, and so on.

WdG: But you have other modifications besides IM, don't you? Aren't you immune to most diseases?

ST: I have one hundred thirty-five genetic modifications besides IM, which were all the ones available when I was born. There have been others since then, but nothing terribly significant.

WdG: What modifications do you have? Can you name some of them?

ST: The important ones are well-known: immunity to HIV and all forms of cancer, a highly-boosted immune system, increased coagulation of the blood, many things like that.

WdG: For survivability.

ST: Sure. But there are others that are less important. Aesthetic modifications, for example.

WdG: But if you have such good immunity, why the concern with disease?

ST: Pathogens mutate over time. It's possible that we could encounter something which our immune systems, plus modern medicine, couldn't counter.

You see, when you do not age, you have to handle risk differently. One's chances of being a victim of a crime or an accident might be, statistically, very low. But the longer one lives, the greater the odds become. One might avoid a car or a plane crash during an eighty-year life. But what about over three hundred, five hundred, a thousand years? One must take extra precautions. That's what Elysium is about. It's an experiment in risk management. And, because it is meant to continue forever, we never reach an outcome. Therefore, immortality can only be a theory.

WdG: How's the experiment been going so far?

ST: We have minor accidents here from time to time, despite precautions. Someone slips and falls. Perhaps cuts themselves. But we've never had an accident that was close to life-threatening.

WdG: I imagine you have a first-rate medical facility here.

ST: The best in the world.

WdG: And I've met your security detail.

ST: Only a fraction of it. I hope they weren't unpleasant to you.

WdG: Not at all. But they didn't seem to be armed.

ST: Those on the island are not. They're called the Aegis. They're martial arts experts. They are brought to the island as toddlers and trained like little Spartans. They are also our emergency responders — in case of medical emergencies or fire, for example.

WdG: Do you believe you can live for a thousand years or more?

ST: I think it's possible. Without aging, it's only a matter of controlling external risks. Some are things we can control through behavior. I can choose not to go swimming, to avoid the risk of drowning. I can make sure I'm inside during a lightning storm. But then, there are many precautions in the ecosystem here. It's all GM life.

WdG: All of it?

ST: Yes. The island is like an organism that fights off infection.

WdG: Infection?

ST: Suppose an insect-borne disease springs up in the future; the flora and fauna of the island would detect and kill foreign animals and bacteria.

WdG: And people?

ST: The Aegis would. They have.

WdG: Terrorists have attacked here?

ST: They never made it ashore.

WdG: I imagine you can't say much about it.

ST: Actually, I couldn't if I wanted to; I'm not on the Committee for Security, so I don't know all that much. But suffice it to say that the Aegis know everything that's happening on and around the island.

WdG: In that case, let's go back to when you first came here.

ST: Things were different here when I arrived, because none of the Immortals were old enough to care for themselves yet. We had nannies to take care of us. And the teachers in our little school. When the IMs were old enough, we took over the teaching roles and began to have our own children. And the mortal teachers were slowly retired. The last one died sixty-two years ago.

WdG: What about mortals who pay to have IM children? I thought everyone on Elysium was supposed to be born of IMs from now on.

ST: There are still some IM children of mortals who come here, but they're increasingly rare. Most of the families of the world who can afford the procedure have had it done.

WdG: How many families?

ST: Two hundred. The corporation knew it wanted the first generation population of Elysium to be around two hundred IMs. They set the price of the procedure so that only the world's richest two hundred families could afford it. That's one way to determine the price of your service…

WdG: Please tell me what it was like when you first came here.

ST: It wasn't much of a shock, because it was not all that different from the life I had been living. I had private tutors at home in Toronto. I had them here, too, although there were also small classes with other immortal students.

WdG: They were all first generation IMs?

ST: Yes. These were all children of mortals. There were about two dozen of us who came here within about a year, when Elysium was first opened to settlement. We stayed in a big communal home. It was like a giant bed and breakfast. And across town were a few classrooms.

The headmaster of the place was an old Welshman named Swansea. He was actually a viscount. Rather harsh man. Discipline, morality. I remember my mother telling me that the parents of the IM children had to take him aside one day and tell him to moderate his tone a bit. He was treating us like mortal children, and it wasn't appropriate. I remember that I thought it was odd that he talked of ethics in terms of God's anger. I knew I was never going to die and meet God anyway.

WdG: You knew you were immortal?

ST: Sure. All of us knew it from a very young age. I remember when my grandmother died. I was nine at the time. I was scared. I asked my mother if I would die, too. If I would lay there like that, looking like a wax figure, and be lowered into the ground. She told me, no, I would never die. She said I was special. Other people had death in them, she said. Even she and my father would die. But I would not. I said I was sad because she would have to die, too. She said it was alright. I would have friends who would never die. One day, all of the people I had known before would be gone, but I would live forever with my friends in a beautiful place. We would always be young and beautiful and have everything we wanted.

WdG: When did your mother pass away?

ST: Seventy years ago. She was eighty.

WdG: And your father?

ST: Five years before her.

WdG: What was daily life like here when you were a child?

ST: With the exception of the headmaster, it was a happy time. There was always something going on. A game or birthday party in the big common room. The residential directors were good to us. They were like communal mothers. Some were the mothers of IM children.

We'd be up and ready for classes by eight. Then we would walk together to the classrooms, which were in the village. The classes were demanding. We all had the modifications for increased intelligence and memory, so they pushed us. Classical literature, fine arts, art history, sociology, political history. Those were requirements. We could choose different classes after that. Science, math, whatever we wanted. We had some of the best teachers in the world. Some from Oxbridge and Harvard.

WdG: Even at a young age?

ST: I was studying Greek drama under Doctor Antovich from Oxford at age fourteen.

WdG: All the professors gave up their lives back in the world?

ST: No. We would meet many of them in the annexes periodically. The best ones didn't come here.

WdG: Could you get degrees at the school?

ST: Yes. Most of us got PhDs in the fine arts.

WdG: Since you were going to stay on Elysium, I assume that these weren't trade-oriented programs.

ST: Not primarily. They had to come up with a unique program for unique people. No, we did not need to work, but what if we wanted to one day? Like my dabbling in architecture. So our early education was designed to teach us two things. First, to give us enough basic knowledge and skills to go on to learn anything we wanted. Second, to give us an understanding of the world and an appreciation of beauty.

WdG: Did you study architecture at the village school or at an annex?

ST: The annex in Paris. I hired Dr. Briere from the Sorbonne. He'd give me the readings, and then we'd meet once a week in the annex. He would test me on the readings and then we'd discuss them.

WdG: Why did you choose architecture?

ST: No deep reason. I liked it. I wanted to try my hand at it.

WdG: You've certainly made a lot of architects jealous of your success.

ST: Thank you.

WdG: Aside from the academics, what else occupied your time when you were growing up here?

ST: Things that occupy all girls, I guess. Birthday parties, dances, boys. Various sports — steeplechase was my favorite. That and fencing. They tried to get me into something more team-oriented, but it never captured my imagination.

WdG: Obviously, your friends from school are here with you now. But your teachers, the mortals, are gone. Do you miss them?

ST: Sometimes. They were good people. Except the headmaster. But as time went on, I think we all got used to the idea that normal people would always just come and go. And society will change, while we will probably retain the cultural norms we were raised with.

WdG: Would you say that's another reason for the isolation of this island? Other than risk management?

ST: Our cultural isolation was not part of the original motivation. But, yes, it makes sense. We are slowly becoming strangers to the world. And I guess everyone would prefer friends they can share their entire life with. For an Immortal, only another Immortal can provide that.

WdG: Who were your closest friends back in school?

ST: Devon, I suppose. She was my suitemate. We didn't get along at first, but we became very close over time. I think that was true for most of us when we first came here. Few of us had siblings, because the price of the procedure is so high. So it was hard for us to get along when we all came together. The resident assistants had their hands full with us for the first year or so as we all learned how to live with strangers and get along. And Devon and I had our little group — Lillian, Antoinette, and Reema.

WdG: No boys?

ST: They had separate quarters, so it took us longer to get close to them. Some of us had boyfriends of sorts while we were at the boarding school and we'd meet them on weekends. But we were discouraged from it. The teachers told us we had infinite time later on for such things, and that we should just concentrate on our studies. Maybe they were just trying to make their own jobs easier. You know, let us deal with boys after they were no longer responsible for us. It must have been very hard for the boys' teachers. A teenage boy is a teenage boy, even if he goes on to live forever.

WdG: Did you have a boyfriend?

ST: Rourke Douglas. We dated on and off. He lives on the other side of the island. But mostly I stayed with our little group. The place was very cliquish, you see. They were always trying to get us to identify with each other. You know, telling us that we needed to get along and help each other, because we were a special group. No matter what happened in the world, we had to work together. No one else in the world would help us. In fact, much of the world was hostile and wanted to hurt us.

We did learn to work together, but that was due to circumstances, I think, more than any indoctrination. We cooperate because it makes sense. And I do think Immortals empathize with each other in a way they simply cannot do with mortals. But the cliques developed in school, and they're still with us now. It's just what people do, I guess.

WdG: You mentioned sports. Did you compete?

ST: Oh yes. Particularly in fencing. My *salle* instructor loved me. He said I was the best student he ever had. Then again, he had never worked with IMs before. The enhancements help in learning anything.

WdG: Did he have other students here?

ST: He taught many of us. Monsieur Talmond was his name. He said even among the Immortals I was the best. I *was* very good, too. I even beat the boys who had much better reach.

WdG: I'm surprised they let you have the swords here.

ST: Foil only. Epée and saber are considered weapons. And a few people practice kendo with bamboo swords.

WdG: How much did you train?

ST: Two hours a day, three days a week. Not that much. But I was also riding when I was not fencing, and most of my time was taken up with studies. Classes and homework.

WdG: Very busy schedule.

ST: There wasn't that much time for anything else. Like socializing. We could leave the program at age eighteen if we wanted to, but it was designed to educate us to twenty-one, when we stopped aging. At that point, most of us had the equivalent of a PhD. Then we'd build a house on the island and move out of the boarding school.

WdG: Did anyone drop out before age twenty-one?

ST: No. There was a strong sense of competition in the school. No one wanted to seem like a failure. The pressure was intense. Our parents had given us the greatest gift that can be given. It had cost the savings of a dynasty. We could have lives like no one else. We could become great artists, scientists, philosophers, whatever we wanted, because we could hone our skills for centuries. Not even savants among mortals could match us. That was the dream our parents had for us. So we all felt it was our duty to repay our parents' generosity. Also, we knew our parents were mortal, and we wanted to make them happy while we could.

WdG: What sort of things have IMs accomplished? I know about your architecture.

ST: Charles Dowers is well-known in the world of philosophy. He does epistemology, particularly regarding postmodern historians. He sometimes gives lectures at the annexes. Sarah Pratchet you've probably heard of. She's the pianist.

WdG: I've seen her on TV.

ST: Wonderful musician. Also a very good composer. We often ask her to play at gatherings here. She's even played fundraisers outside the annexes.

WdG: For whom?

ST: The International Order of Doctors.

WdG: I know Graham Wiloczki has become quite famous.

ST: Yes. And he never leaves the island. He ships his paintings out to galleries and shows. And there's Young-Il Chen; she's an economic theorist. She's worked for the United Nations.

WdG: How did you get the Louvre job?

ST: I simply submitted my concepts. And I had done the Kolowski Museum, too, so that was on my résumé.

I think Briere probably put in a good word for me. I hope I won on my own merit, but the literature about the museum made much of the fact that I'm from Elysium. I think there was an element of mystery in that for them. At least that's how it seems from their ad copy.

WdG: You know what occurred to me while you were talking about everyone's art…it seems that so many artists want their art to be a form of immortality.

ST: True. But I guess IM artists and craftsmen have a different motivation, since we already have immortality.

WdG: What is it?

ST: Maybe it's just love of art.

Chapter 5

THE NEXT MORNING, after breakfast, Sophia suggested we visit the village so she could show me around. A chauffer drove us down the hill and into the square I'd passed when I first arrived, and opened the doors for us by the fountain. This time I noticed there was nothing mundane to ruin the magic of the village. There were no trash cans, no power lines, no antennas or solar panels. Every building was a work of art.

We strolled the wide sidewalks under the shade trees, and the sea breeze moderated the Mediterranean heat. There were a few people on the sidewalks. I bid one of them good morning as we passed, but he did not look at me. The streets were full of restaurants, cafés, and bakeries; there was also a theatre, an antiquarian bookstore, and several boutiques full of what I assumed were the latest fashions.

"These places don't pay for themselves, do they?" I asked Sophia.

"No. They're supported by the corporation. They're just here to provide some entertainment for us. If we want something in particular, it can be flown in."

"And the people working in them?"

"Same as the menservants and cooks — they're from the outside. Like the maintenance staff."

"I haven't seen any maintenance staff. But the place is spotless."

"They generally work at night. But they are watching all the time, and would go to work if it was necessary."

"If it's rare for an Immortal to be born now, then the corporation must be paying for everything through its investments."

"It still does modification work for mortals," said Sophia. "But you're right in guessing that most of its income is from investment."

"Investment strategy must look a little different if you're planning for eternal life."

"We have the best economists in the world," she said. "And yes, our investments are meant for the long-term. Even simple compound interest over such long periods of time is very lucrative, given the large initial investments the corporation made."

"What happens if the world economy collapses? Could IMs survive?"

"There are contingency plans. The investments are so large and diversified that we could continue functioning through a major disruption. Also, through our political connections, we would do everything we could do to prevent a breakdown."

"You have that much influence?"

"Certainly. The money is part of it. But governments like to deal with Immortals because we'll always be here, the same people, the same personalities. A refuge of stability in an unstable world, decade after decade."

We came to a small nook set in an alley between two buildings. There were two seats of stone and brass facing a white wall, the whole affair made private by a cordon of small, pink-flowered myrtles.

She sat in one of the chairs and asked, "What would you like to see?"

I sat next to her. "Like what?"

"Anything at all."

"Today's financial headlines," I said.

The wall illuminated and showed us a program of the latest stock market results with a commentary playing through hidden speakers.

"Beethoven's 9th, last movement," I said. The screen gave me a few options of sound and video recordings, and I chose a video clip from the Copenhagen Philharmonic.

We watched a few more items — interactive museum tours, including one of Sophia's in Warsaw, more music, a little history, and a map of Elysium.

"There's a walking path down by the harbor," I said, studying the map.

"Would you like to see it?"

"Please."

We walked down to the harbor under the shade trees. It was like a botanical garden, with reflecting pools and statues along the way. There were a few sailboats and a large yacht in the harbor. There were boathouses and open, airy cafés and restaurants along the water. I'd been to Capri and Funchal, but they were no match for the beauty of this town, especially since it was spotless and there were only a few people to be seen.

We walked around the edge of the harbor to the beach. The landscape was much wilder although equally beautiful. The path wound between rocks above a narrow beach, and through groves of mountain laurel and Japanese maples. Aside from the path, there was not a sign of civilization, although I guessed that eyes or other devices had been fixed on me since my arrival. Not without reason, I thought. Although I had passed the corporation's background checks, there was no way for Sophia to know if my sympathies lay with her enemies. The contacts I'd made with militant groups in the course of my career had no doubt set off alarms within the corporation. How could they, or Sophia, be sure I had not come to kill someone? I don't know if I could've done it in Sophia's home, where I slept in a guest room. Maybe some of the servants were actually Aegis. But out here we were alone, and I knew I could've killed her had I wanted. Getting away might have been impossible, but there are plenty of people who don't care about that. Maybe she knew something I didn't. We sat on a rock overlooking the sea.

"Are the annexes this lovely?" I asked.

"They're luxurious, but not very big. They're always enclosed by walls. Kind of claustrophobic."

"Is that why you like to travel outside the annexes?"

"I try to keep that to a minimum because of the danger. Still, sometimes I get a sort of cabin fever and need to see something new. And do something…challenging."

"Like going to war zones with journalists?"

"I hope so. I've never done anything that radical, though."

"What's the most radical thing you've done?" In retrospect, that was pretty daring.

"Well…Rourke and I were in the annex in Rome just before we defended our dissertations. I went for some final research, and he said he needed to go to the National Archives for his own dissertation. It seemed to me that the documents he wanted from the archives were tangential, at best, to his research. I think he just wanted to be in Rome with me.

"We had dated on and off since we were sixteen. Nothing much, since the boys and girls were pretty much separate from each other at the boarding school. You know, we'd sneak out sometimes at night if we could get away with it.

"But when we were in Rome we were already older, and the teachers didn't watch us much anymore. We wore tracking devices, but we had to activate them in order for anyone to know where we were. We could order an Aegis escort outside the annex if we wanted, but it wasn't required.

"One night Rourke comes around while I'm having dinner. He asked me if I wanted to go out that night. I asked him where he wanted to go. I was suspicious, because he always wanted to go someplace just for sex. He usually wasn't successful with me, but he was certainly persistent. He said he'd read about a dance club outside of town and wanted to go see it. It sounded interesting. I had never been to such a place, and was curious to know what it was like. He made it sound like Nirvana, so we went out that night to find it.

"He dressed in a leather jacket, an old-fashioned cotton shirt with a high, starched collar, and black slacks with embroidery down the sides. I have no idea if it was considered chic. I just wore a little black dress.

"We took a cab to the edge of town and decided to walk around to find the place. He didn't know exactly where it was, only the neighborhood. But the neighborhood did not look at all friendly. Abandoned buildings. Trash everywhere. I'd never seen a place like that. I'd look up into the windows and see torn curtains billowing out, or a broken pane, or a bare bulb on a ceiling and think, I can't believe people actually live in a place like this. The horses in my stables have better accommodations.

"I told Rourke I wanted to go back, but he said he wanted to find the club. Once we found the club, we'd be fine. I said it was clearly dangerous, and he said it was okay because he was armed. He said one of the Aegis had given him a gun, which I knew was nonsense. Nor did it make me feel any safer.

"Just as I was going to call a cab for myself, we saw people going in and out of a decrepit building. We could hear music whenever someone opened the door. Rourke said that must be it. I said it can't be; it's just an old factory. Like everything else there, it looked like it was falling apart. But he took me by the arm and pulled me in with him.

"It was a dance club after all, but not a legal one. More like a speakeasy. The kids had just moved into an abandoned building and set up powerful amplifiers and lights. It was hard to see anything in there, and the music was deafening. It never stopped. It was a sort that seemed to be the same thing over and over. When the lights flashed, I could see the faces. I can't really describe them. It was like a dance club in *Divine Comedy*. Their clothes and hair, the tattoos and everything. It wasn't from this world.

"Rourke wanted to dance, but I wanted to just look around. So he danced with some girls, if that's what they were, and I walked around, which wasn't easy for me in the dark with flashing lights. I was scared, but fascinated. Every time the lights changed, I saw something else. There was a packing crate with candles on it. In the crate were bottles, and some of the boys took the bottles from the open side of the crate and either drank from them or sold them. In a corner, people were dancing and swallowing pills with wine or whatever it was. Some were having sex with half their clothes on. There were others lying along the wall like they were dead. I didn't think things like that happened anywhere in the world.

"Then some boys were dancing around me like I was a maypole. They followed along with me as I walked. But then they stopped me. When I tried to move they blocked my path. When I tried to push past them they pushed me back into the circle. Then their hands were on me. They kept dancing the whole time and some were just touching me and others were lifting up my dress. No one seemed to notice. I thought, there are no police here, no Aegis. I could hit the panic button on my watch, but how long would it take for anyone to reach me? They would just carry my corpse out.

"I slapped one of them — the only time I've ever hit anyone. He just laughed. Then they stopped dancing and tried to pull me into another room. I screamed, but I don't think anyone could hear me over the music. Maybe they didn't care.

"Then Rourke runs up and pushes one of them. They all drew knives. I could see the lights reflecting off them. And then Rourke had a gun in his hand. I was surprised he actually had one. One of them dared him to shoot, and he did. It lit the place like a camera flash, and the report was louder than the music. He missed and the shot cratered the wall and showered everyone with bits of concrete. It was the only thing in the room that turned heads that night.

"Then he froze. They either ran or threw their hands up. I grabbed his arm and pulled him out the door with me. We went around the corner and I called a cab. It picked us up, and on the ride back he was angry because I seemed ungrateful that he'd saved my life. Playing the hero. Was I okay? Oh, I was lucky he showed up when he did. Never should've left his side in the first place. I told him not to talk about it. Ever. I didn't think he would, not with the gun. God only knows where he got it. Not in the annex. But maybe he would brag to his friends. Maybe telling stories of braving the concrete jungle over his tea and brioche the next morning. I was brushing concrete dust off me and trying to get the bits out of my hair. He had the taxi drop us near the annex, and then dropped the gun in a drain grate. I'm not sure if he talked about it to anyone. At least it never came back to me."

"You got lucky," I said.

"He should never have taken me down there in the first place."

"You did sorta enjoy it, didn't you? Especially when you thought about it afterwards?"

"Well…yes," she said with an embarrassed smile. "But you're the only person I know who would understand that."

"Did you ever talk to him after that?"

"Sure. Not about that night, though. We've served on committees for the corporation together. Even dated on and off. But never talked about that night in Rome."

"You've dated him on and off for ninety-four years?"

"Yes. Others too."

"That reminds me. I wanted to ask you about marriage among Immortals," I said. "You don't have "til death do us part.""

"I don't think anyone here is married at this point," she said. "It doesn't make any sense. There's no economic need."

"Raising kids?"

"We don't need help. We all have servants, and we can get tutors if we want them. The traditional nuclear family doesn't make much sense here. But it was a problem for our parents. They were generally from very conservative families. The idea of their children remaining single wasn't considered, and the idea of having children outside wedlock was anathema to them. So they pressured most of the IMs to marry.

"Everyone could see the problems with it. Wouldn't you get tired of the same person after the first five hundred years?"

I silently wondered if I'd become tired of *myself* after five hundred years.

"No mortal is asked to put up with someone for so long, to be infinitely patient," Sophia continued. "Also, there is no need for someone to inherit the family name or fortune. Our parents appreciated all this, but, for most of them, their upbringing was too much and they insisted on marriage. To another Immortal, naturally, which limited the potential pool. Luckily, some people in the corporation suggested that IMs all sign prenuptial agreements beforehand. It's a good thing they did, because every couple divorced after their parents died. The prenuptials prevented embarrassing fights. Their parents were even against those, before giving in."

"Did any of those couples have children before divorcing?"

"Yes. It did complicate things a bit. But, like I said, we avoid serious problems because we know that we all have to live together on this island."

"Do IMs have to pay to have the procedure performed on their own children?"

"No," said Sophia. "We are allowed to have one child per female, no charge. If you want more, the corporation has to approve their living on Elysium. Even if it does, you'd have to pay for the procedure. And the female reproductive system would have to be activated through drugs first. It's not active otherwise. It's a form of birth control."

"You could still have a mortal child, couldn't you?"

"Yes. But no one would bring a mortal into the world. Who would want to watch their child die?"

No one, I thought, although in the places Sophia wanted to visit with me, they did it quite often.

"Have you ever married?" she asked.

"No."

"Why not?"

"Never met the right person," I said. "Plus I'm not sure it's a good idea with this lifestyle."

"The constant travel?"

"Yeah. And anyway, I never wanted children, so marriage didn't have much appeal."

"Don't you get lonely?"

"Sure."

"It can't be easy. You have to face all that stress without any emotional support."

"True."

"Unless…"

"Unless I just find emotional support wherever I can," I said.

"Like who?"

"Like whoever doesn't get out of the way fast enough."

"Now, I told you about Rourke."

"Yeah, and you didn't even tell me to strike it from the record."

"Oh yes. I forgot you're a journalist."

"Thank you."

"But no doubt you've got some stories you haven't reported."

"Well...what can I tell you?"

"Something romantic..."

I thought about it for a moment. I had plenty of stories, but wasn't sure what she considered 'romantic.' It could be a problem if I said something that didn't fit her definition.

"I was leaving El Salvador," I said. "This was about ten years ago. I had been working on a story for the Associated Press. Covering the coastal rebellion. But the guerillas thought I was a foreign spy, so I had to beat it back to San Salvador. When I got there, the government decided I was working for the guerillas as a propagandist. They wanted to arrest me, but the embassy intervened, so the government just declared me *persona non grata* and gave me seventy-two hours to leave the country.

"I booked a flight to Mexico City and made a quick trip to the countryside to find someone. Got back just in time to catch my flight.

"So I got on the plane and Lucia sat next to me. She was an environmental scientist from Mexico City who'd worked on a desalinization project in El Salvador and was going home now. We talked the whole way about the social problems in El Salvador; she knew everything there was to know about their environmental economy. Outgoing, friendly. I'm surprised she had anything to do with me in the state I was in. I hadn't washed in several days, I think."

"What did Lucia look like?" asked Sophia.

"She was twenty-five to my thirty at the time. She came up to my nose and had long brown hair which she usually kept pulled back, sometimes braided. Her eyes were tan. She was in very good shape, because she spent so much time working in the field and liked to hike.

"We talked the whole way. I'd planned on taking a flight from Mexico City to New York, but by the time we landed, we were going to the Pacific Coast together. She knew a lot about the insurgency I'd been covering, and what I'd seen. So I guess she figured I was in bad shape and needed some help. She was right, too."

"Don't you get used to it?"

"No," I said. "Or, at least, I never have. Maybe I'd give it up if I got used to it. But when we landed, we rented a car and drove seven hours to a *reconstruido* south of Acapulco called Playa Valiente. Do you know what a *reconstruido* is?"

"A town rebuilt after the original was flooded by rising sea levels," said Sophia.

"Right. And in Mexico they're often populated by people from further inland who couldn't find work in the cities. When we got there, I still hadn't slept or eaten right, and the people looked at me a bit oddly. Plus I was the only foreigner in town at the time. Lucia knew a family there; that's how she knew it was a good place to disappear for a while.

"It was just a little village, maybe five hundred people. There was a small restaurant and a bar at the crossroads. There was also a restaurant above the beach called the Bolumba. It did a fairly good business with the city tourists who sometimes came through, trying to get some clean air. It had a few palm *cabañas* next to it. Lucia and I rented one for ourselves. It had no electricity or running water. We used the toilets, sinks, and showers at the restaurant. I remember the toilets were in a shack behind the restaurant, and the sinks were on the wall outside, so everyone could watch you brush your teeth. The shower was just a head sticking out of the wall of the outhouse with a wooden fence around it. I remember all the tile had been salvaged from other buildings and patched together like a mosaic. It was always full of beach sand, and there were small orange lizards on the walls. Oh yeah, and the toilet didn't have a seat.

"The restaurant was one small building, the kitchen and the bar together, with all the plastic tables and chairs on a patio under a terra cotta roof. The floor was beach sand.

"The first thing I did when we moved into our little *cabaña* was strip naked and jump in the ocean. I swam for an hour and scrubbed my body with beach sand. Then I went back and slept in the *cabaña* for about fourteen hours, until the next morning. Lucia's friends had lent us a heavy Indian rug to sleep on, and some fleece blankets.

"I guess Lucia slept next to me, but she was gone when I woke up. There were some clothes next to me, some second-hand shirts and pants from Lucia's friends. I went for a short swim, dried off, dressed, and went up to the Bolumba. Luis was in charge in the mornings. He'd make me all kinds of wonderful breakfasts, usually with fruit or seafood. Always fresh. Everything from local farms. My favorite was eggs and *chorizo*, with mangos sprinkled with lime juice. And excellent coffee.

"I was there for two weeks with Lucia. We spent all the days together. We hiked all up and down the coast and talked about everything. Politics, things we'd seen, our childhoods. I bought a rod and reel in town, and we'd fish in the surf. Sometimes we'd cook what we caught over a bonfire on the beach. Or if it was late we'd bring it back to the Bolumba and have Mario cook it for us. Mario ran the place in the evenings. He had kinky-curly black hair and a gold tooth. And you saw it a lot because he was always laughing. He was the happiest person I ever met, and he made margaritas like he meant to use up all the tequila before I left. Sometimes before dinner I'd go into the kitchen and help them cook. The women in the kitchen were stoic and never said anything when I got there. Some of them were pure Indian and didn't speak any Spanish. They didn't know what to make of me when I offered to help in the kitchen. But I carried the bags of cornmeal and the buckets of water, and I even knew how to mix and knead the cornmeal and make tamales. Then they liked me and always laughed when they saw a man, and a foreigner, washing dishes. All the foreigners they'd seen had been on vacation and never wanted to do anything but eat and drink and lay in the sun. They started calling me *El Cocinero Gringo*. One of the women offered to wash my dirty clothes from El Salvador for a couple of dollars. She washed them in a pot that we usually used to boil corn; then she rinsed them in sea water and hung them to dry on a line over the patio. They were stiff when I put them on, and the coarse cotton hurt my sunburn. I was pretty dark by then, and the ladies changed my name to *El Cocinero Mexicano*.

"Lucia and I would often go to her friends' house for dinner. They were a great bunch. They lived in Mexico City, but this was their summer home. We made a couple trips up the coast with them, and into the tiny downtown sometimes in the evening. None of the roads were paved, and *burros* and pigs were always wandering around. The whole town looked like it was rebuilt from leftover bits of other towns, but it was alive. People were selling roasted chicken along the road and the children were running and laughing everywhere. It was only poor in terms of money.

"I was pretty sick of life and people and the world when I left El Salvador. But it was starting to lift now. I had to see that there were still places in the world that were sane and peaceful. Still people who weren't killing and dying. And Lucia and I slept together curled up like two trusting kittens."

"You didn't have sex with her?"

"Not until the end. It wasn't what I wanted or needed. But then she needed to go back to Mexico City. That last night in Playa Valiente we had our blankets out on the beach and watched the waves in the moonlight. Then we were making love. Neither of us said a word. Afterward we slept on the beach. In the morning we got in the car and drove back to Mexico City. She dropped me off at the airport and we said goodbye."

"That was it?"

"That was it. Just an event. Just two people. We connected for a while, and then went our own ways."

"Didn't you stay in touch with her?"

"No. I know I could've. But I guess both of us had learned by then how people come and go in life, especially lives like ours. We might exchange a few messages, then other things and other people would intervene, and we'd forget each other anyway. So we just let it go."

"You'll never see her again?"

"Probably not."

"I can't imagine that," said Sophia. "Everything just crumbles for you."

"Never a dull moment," I said.

"I'm sure. But that's not the problem. What you can't have is stability. You know, IMs don't suffer from mental illnesses, not even common neurosis. There are mods against psychosis, but not neurosis. But we don't suffer from them, either, because of our stability. We have security. We don't strain to get control of our situations."

"Do you feel that's what neurosis is about?"

"I think most of it is. But there's the catch. Mortals can never get control of their lives. The only thing a mortal can do is try to accept the insanity of his situation. Mortal life is inherently flawed. Mortals form attachments to each other, of course they do, but they can't keep them, because they die or otherwise change. Their bodies and minds change, and they can't control them. They need control to have security, but they can never get complete control, because their lives are unstable. Mortal life is about a deep-seated drive to get something that you absolutely never can get. Mortal life is a failure. It is a mistake. It is inescapably painful and meaningless.

"Immortals don't suffer, because they have attained control over their own existences. We have conquered the world. We have conquered life itself. Life is shaped by us, not the other way around. I imagine this sounds arrogant to you. But remember that you're in a different world now. France is only nine kilometers away. You can see the coast from the north beach. But Elysium is more profoundly different from France than is the surface of the moon. Because the reality is different, our philosophical foundations are different, and so our ethics are different."

We stayed on the cliffs above the beach talking for a few hours, and watched the sun setting over the water; then we went back to the village, where Sophia's driver picked us up and took us back to her home.

Chapter 6

THE NEXT MORNING, Sophia and I had breakfast together before going riding. In the dining room I was served braised eggs and fresh croissants, *café con leche*, tropical fruits with flavored yogurt, and warm, fresh dark bread with duck pâté. The china was gold-rimmed. We ate the eggs with silver spoons, and the instruments to spread the pâté, I remember, looked like tiny oars of teak.

"Do you have a garden here?" I asked.

"Yes, out back. Just a hectare. I toy with it now and then. The staff does most of the work. I also have some chickens and geese."

"Everything I've had here is so fresh…it must all come from your garden."

"Oh, no," she said. "We grow quite a bit on the island, and on the next one over, in our communal gardens. Part of that is for security and quality control. But most of the food is imported daily from the mainland. And there are the bakeries in the village."

After breakfast we rode her genetically-perfect horses in the hills above the town, through groves of redbud and dogwood. The hills were not high, only a hundred meters or so. We came to an overlook above a field bordered by hydrangeas. In the field were about a dozen people, some playing instruments, some dancing, others singing. Their laughter reached us even at this distance. I came alongside Sophia.

"*Affinitas*," she said. "It's a game of relationships. Someone opens with a theme expressed in dance, or music, or poetry. Maybe with mathematics or sketching. The next person performs an expression of a related concept, and the one before him must guess the relationship. There are no set rules. Just what people agree upon at the start."

"Do you play?"

"Sure. We all do. I'm not the best, though. I've been known to lose a bet."

"You bet on *Affinitas*?"

"Well, it started off as *Affinitas*," she said. "But Winslow challenged me to a poetry duel halfway through. It was the duel I lost."

"What's a poetry duel?"

"A competition in which each person composes a poem in a set period of time, which is usually very brief. Sometimes there's a preset theme. A third party judges the winner."

"What did you play for?"

"My body. He wanted me bad, the little snot. Against a first edition of Piranesi's *Roman Antiquities*. Definitely worth more than one night with me.

"But the judge went against me, and in the evening Winslow took me to a cliff above the ocean. I remember that the stars were very bright and clear, and we could see the lights of Cap Bénat on the horizon. It was chilly and I didn't want to undress. I was angry with him, but I had to keep my word. But after a while I started to enjoy it, and it turned out to be a nice night after all."

Strip poker poetry, I thought, and decided not to say that out loud.

We were riding side-by-side now. "What other pastimes do you have here? Do you mind if I record this?"

"No, I don't mind."

* * *

WdG: Sophia Trevelyan and I are discussing pastimes here on Elysium. We've discussed *Affinitas* and, uh, poetry duels. What else do you have?

ST: Lots of concerts. Poetry recitals. Some sporting events – fencing, polo, tennis, all kinds. Picnics. Theatre. Lectures on various topics. Art exhibits. Dinner parties. Dances…

WdG: Art exhibits from the outside?

ST: Rarely. They're usually put on by residents. There are a lot of ways to occupy your time here. Good books. Gardening, when I want it, and riding. Swimming, though I usually stay in the pool rather than go down to the beaches. Snorkeling. Photography. Cinema. Restaurants in the village. Sometimes someone will organize a high-stakes game of poker or baccarat. Hiking in the hills. Some of us like to dabble in cooking and then invite taste testers over. Beach parties around a bonfire at night. Sometimes just lying on the beach talking, or doing nothing at all.

WdG: You mentioned certain responsibilities, like the committees.

ST: Yes. They're not requirements, but since we're all in this together, it's good to participate. There are committees for Security, French Relations, Investments, and so on. But I probably shouldn't say too much about them.

WdG: How much of your time do the committees take?

ST: Not much. Day-to-day affairs are handled by the servants. The Aegis pretty much look after themselves, but they answer to the Committee for Security. I'm on the committees for Investments and Land Use. I might put in ten hours a month. Nothing much.

WdG: How much time do you give to architecture?

ST: Only a little, unless I'm trying to win a contract. And I only submit plans when I feel like it. Most of the time I'm just dabbling, researching, getting new ideas. Sometimes I'll attend a conference outside the annexes. Maybe go to a show as long as I'm out. Like when we met in Quebec.

On occasion I'll take a long trip outside the annexes. Travel for a few weeks, I mean. That requires a lot of security arrangements, though. When we travel outside the annexes, it's usually to Paris, Marseille, or Saint Tropez, because we have standing arrangements in those places. I used to enjoy going to Saint Tropez and dancing in the kind of clubs that no one would want here. But usually I just stay here now. I think most of us do. It's easier to import the things we like, rather than export ourselves.

* * *

We rode along a ridge for a few minutes, then turned downhill into a small grotto. There was a low cliff, perhaps ten feet high and twenty feet long. There was a figure carved into the cliff face, projecting outward, like a bas relief trying to step out of the wall. The main component was the head and torso of an androgynous figure, but it was combined with diverse shapes – religious icons, zodiacal signs, archetypical symbols, and other things I didn't recognize. The varying textures and hues in the sculpture came from the different types of rock from which it was composed, and were of such variety that I doubted they existed naturally in one place.

We sat, still mounted, in front of the sculpture and stared silently. The face of the sculpture bore a sublime expression, as if in ecstasy, but still pining for a state yet unachieved. The entire structure was asymmetrical and somehow extremely compelling. I had the odd impression it was actually located in my mind and not the cliff. It hinted at some inconceivable blending of the intellectual and the irrational, a nexus of these two streams of human experience. It seemed to speak to a part of my mind hidden from view, and I sensed a potential energy, contained but not suppressed, of something yet to come.

We sat silently for a long time. Finally my horse shook its head and I realized again where I was.

"Amazing," I said.

"Isn't it?"

"I've never seen anything like it."

"Rachael is the greatest sculptor in the world."

"She gets my vote."

"This is what I'd like to do with architecture," she said. "I want to create spaces that do similar things to people who enter them, to activate aspects of the subconscious just by being in them. Could be interesting for, say, a university, or a hall of congress. It would be exponentially more difficult in a building, because of the constraints imposed by function. But one day I'll do it. I have time."

I followed her as she rode on from the sculpture, back uphill to the summit and along the ridge, with its view of the sea, to another trail which turned downhill towards the interior of the island. We entered a narrow valley or clove; I was surprised it was so deep, given that the hills on the island were not very high. The trail descended halfway into the valley to an outcropping, covered in thick grass, hanging over the gorge. We rode onto the outcropping and dismounted.

I sat on the grass next to the horses while Sophia walked to the edge of the drop. It was here I saw most clearly that the vegetation on the island wasn't indigenous; I had seen photographs of the island before the corporation purchased it and, although beautiful, the original trees and bushes were of a drier variety, similar to those of Australia or the American Southwest. But it was lush, almost tropical, here. The valley was partially covered in mist, with patches of wispy cloud hanging in the air, shading the Mediterranean sun, and the breeze from the valley was cool and damp. To the left, a waterfall hung like a satin curtain from the top of the gorge; ivy, ixora, and mimosas clung to the valley walls.

Sophia removed the band at the back of her head and let down her hair. She stood at the edge of the outcropping like a queen surveying her domain.

"Beautiful," I said.

"Sayyid made it."

"Made what?"

"The valley."

"He made the *valley?*"

"Sure. I guess you'd say he's a landscaper."

A rising breeze blew white flowers from the trees into the gorge, where they floated down like snow. A large bird, shaped like a heron but colored like a macaw, took wing and flew across the valley as the breeze reached us, scented with a subtle perfume of faraway flowers.

Still looking out from her perch, Sophia sang in her lovely voice at a slow tempo:

> Now is the month of maying,
> When merry lads are playing, fa la,
> Each with his bonny lass
> Upon the scented grass, fa la.
> The spring, clad in gladness,
> Doth laugh at winter's sadness, fa la,

And to the piper's sound
The nymphs tread out their ground, fa la.
    Fie! why sit we musing,
Youth's sweet delight refusing, fa la.
Say, dainty nymphs, speak:
Shall we play at barley-break? Fa la.

I lay back in the grass, closed my eyes, and listened to the sounds of the valley. Sophia was silent now. I tried to imagine what it was like for her here. Not just in terms of the daily round we'd been discussing, but how she experienced it all. For me, this wasn't Elysium. It had to end. I would go back to work sooner or later in places that were less than heavenly. Even if I could remain here, I would age, decay, and die.

But for Sophia? She believed this would continue forever, and not without reason. No work, no worries. No wondering if the paycheck would clear in time to cover the rent check or if your medical insurance would pay for your treatment. No worries about whether or not a spouse was true to you. There were people in my world who didn't worry about those things, but they did worry about dying. Maybe they raged against it, or maybe they went quietly, but the end was the same. For Sophia, life and beauty were her end and her fate. She had reached a perfect and changeless state.

As I lay listening to the wind in the trees, I felt something very slightly wrong, coming from the same place the statue had accessed. Maybe, I thought, it was the impermanence and death which I carried around inside me, the terminal condition of every cell in my body. Or maybe not.

Chapter 7
Sophia's Transcripts, Part II

WDG: MAY 7, 2175, 1100 HOURS. At the residence of Sophia Trevelyan, continuing interviews. Today, I would like to talk more about your childhood.

ST: Okay.

WdG: You said you were still a child when you had your first encounter with death. And became aware of your own immortality.

ST: Well, I was referring to the first time it was made explicit to me. I remember death appearing only at a distance, as an idea. Once I saw a news story about a famine in Southeast Asia. My mother was in the room at the time. I was seven, I think. I guess I looked disturbed at what I'd seen. She said, "Oh, you don't need to worry about such things," and turned off the screen.

Then, when I was nine, my mother told me we were going to take a trip to visit with my grandmother. My parents had been talking about her in hushed tones for a month. I knew something was wrong. I once asked if everything was alright with Grandmom, and they looked at each other as if they'd been caught. So I knew something was wrong, and that I wasn't supposed to know about it.

My grandmother lived with her servants outside Ottawa. My mother told me we would stay for a few days. We had done this before, but there was no cheerfulness around it this time. My father drove us and everyone was very quiet.

When we got there, Grandmom was in her big chair with lots of blankets on her. The servants were there, but also people I didn't know, wearing some sort of uniform. I guess they were nurses or doctors. My parents went over to see her and knelt by her chair. My mother and grandmother were crying and my father's face was strained and stony. The nurses, or whoever they were, went about their business without looking at us. My mother called me over — I had been standing next to the suitcases — and my grandmother hugged me as best she could from the chair and kissed my cheek.

"Ah, little Sophia," she said.

"What's wrong, Grandmom?" I asked.

She tightened herself up, like she was trying to hold something in. She just shook her head as she cried.

My father went to speak to the nurses in low tones, and my mother walked away so I wouldn't see her crying. My grandmother squeezed my hand. I didn't know what to do. No one would tell me what was wrong, so I didn't understand.

The next day I saw my grandmother again and she seemed very tired, but also more relaxed. We talked for a little while, just about my cousins or uncles and aunts and what they were doing. Just small talk. I remember I was a bit angry at everyone for keeping me in the dark. But I didn't say anything. I could see she was ill and thought that, given her age, she might be dying. But I only knew that theoretically. I had never known anyone who had died.

The next morning, when I woke, I got dressed and went downstairs. My parents were in the parlor. My mother was crying. The servants would appear in a doorway and their eyes were red.

"Oh, honey," my mother called when she saw me. I went to her and she hugged me. When she stopped crying she said, "Your grandmother is in heaven now with your grandfather."

I stood there while my mother cried and my father held her, which was something I'd rarely seen him do. Eventually my father sent me to the dining room to have breakfast by myself. As I walked away, I heard my mother quietly say, "She doesn't understand."

That day, and the next, virtually the entire family arrived. Grandmom had a big chateau and most everyone was able to stay there, although by the second day people were starting to stay at hotels and come to visit. There were dozens of people, and everyone was well-dressed, and the women were crying. The servants, who looked exhausted, were running around trying to feed everyone and carry their bags. It took the attention off me, which I liked. It felt strange to be in my grandmother's home without her there. All the adults were hugging and kissing me and saying things like "Oh, God bless you, my little dear!" But some of them hung back from me, especially the older cousins. Sometimes I noticed them looking at me, whispering. So many things I didn't understand, all at once. So I retreated into propriety. My parents were raising me to be polite and formal. I knew how to do it. So I behaved perfectly, said what I thought was correct, and otherwise remained silent.

On the fourth day was the viewing. It was probably the worst day of my life, except for the day my mother died. My mother had packed a lot of formalwear for me — very lacey, very French — and I sat in the corner with my rosaries. All day long in the parlor everyone came to see Grandmom, who was in a casket at the end of the room. It was surrounded by flowers, and the family crest hung over it. My mother had very little time for me that day. She was the oldest child and was in charge. Sometimes people came over to me to say hello and tell me that I looked pretty. Otherwise, I sat there and pretended to pray the entire day. And I remember thinking that Grandmom was going to have to wake up sooner or later. Because she simply looked asleep in her favorite dress, surrounded by flowers.

In the evening, a priest came and we all said the rosary together before the casket. Then everyone went to bed. I was awake most of the night. I remember thinking that I wanted to go see Grandmom in the night when no one was there, but that my mother would not approve, so I didn't.

The next day was the funeral at the cathedral. It seemed the entire parish turned out for it. The place was awash in flowers. It was a full mass, with a choir and the Knights of Columbus. During the homily, the priest said that this was the moment of refuge for true believers. For non-believers, there was no consolation. Only the faithful could be steadfast at such a time. When they took the casket away, the Knights of Columbus draped a flag over it; but it wasn't the Lamb of God, it was the family crest, with the fleurs-de-lis.

We drove to the cemetery, and there was another ceremony in front of the mausoleum. I'd rarely seen people crying, especially adults. Now everyone was crying. People came up and laid flowers on the casket, and pretty soon the casket was completely covered in beautiful bouquets. I laid my lilies on as I'd seen everyone else do. Then we went back to the chateau for lunch. That was the biggest gathering of my family I had ever seen, and we used to have reunions every five years.

The lunch was much more relaxed. There was even some laughter. My father, who looked very tired, put his hand on my head and said, "You did so well, Sophia. Those were long days for you."

I was watching my mother and waited for her to go outside alone. She always did that during family gatherings. She needed a few minutes to get away from it all. I saw her go out, and slipped off my chair and followed her.

She went into the garden behind the house and stood behind the rose bushes. She smiled when she saw me.

Little Sophia, she said. You've been so good these past few days. This must be so strange for you.

I hugged her and she said, I know you don't understand.

Grandmom is dead, I said.

She's in heaven with Granddad, she said. And they are looking down on all of us now. You can still talk to them. You can pray to them. They are angels now.

But I'll never see her again, I said.

I wish she was here too, honey.

Why do you wish she was here if she's in heaven? I asked.

It was something my mother struggled with. You know, I had all the intelligence mods. I was inexperienced, but I could figure things out much faster than other children of my age. It made it harder for my mother to raise me, I think.

I guess that's just the way we are, Sophia, she said. She looked worn-out.

You're different, though, she said. Her voice was different. Why?

You won't die like the rest of us. You're special.

Why?

Because daddy and I decided to make you that way. You will never die. You won't get old, either.

I thought about it. Are there other girls like me? I asked.

Yes, she said. You'll meet them someday. And you'll live with them in a beautiful place, like heaven. She took my hand and led me back inside. It's probably best if you didn't talk about that with anyone, she said. It's a very special treasure you have. People might be jealous if you talk about it. Alright? Alright, I said.

Now, after I learned more about immortality, I saw the problem with this. If we were all going to heaven when we died, and see our loved ones, our dearly departed, why did they pay for my immortality? Hadn't they denied me heaven? But I didn't say anything, because they had chosen it for me. Wouldn't it be an insult to question their judgment? So I let it go.

WDG: You never asked?

ST: No. But, soon enough, I didn't have to. While I was living at home, my education was very basic. That changed when I got to Elysium. I had access to all the volumes in the library — well, everything in the world, really. So I studied death. Social attitudes, philosophical approaches, theology, everything. And finally I came to the conclusion that our immortality was due to our parents' lack of deep religious conviction. They believed in heaven because human beings are terrified of death. People recognize instinctively that death means the end of the ego-self. So they invent religion as a means of coping. They create the idea of a soul which lasts forever. Theologians have theories about the soul, but most people believe that the soul is the ego-self. That is, the entity that sees through the eyes, has thoughts, feels emotion, and so on. And so they have created the idea of immortality for themselves. The body dies, but the ego-self, the 'me,' does not. And if you were good, not only did you survive, but you also ascend to a paradisal realm for all eternity.

WdG: But then why didn't your parents allow you to go to heaven?

ST: There's only one possibility: they didn't really believe in it. If it is true, wouldn't it be better to spend eternity in the presence of God, rather than on Earth, no matter how good the circumstances? Certainly. But I think they accepted the illusion of the survival of the ego for themselves as an analgesic. Lovely thing. But not for me. Do you know what Pascal's Wager is?

WdG: I don't remember what it says.

ST: It's a logical persuasion for belief in God. It says that if there is a God, you will live forever if you believe in Him. If God does not exist, you don't lose anything by believing in Him, because you would just die anyway. Therefore, it is logical to risk believing in God, because you might gain something.

WdG: Sensible, in a way.

ST: In a businesslike way. I give faith, I might get eternal life. A very good exchange! But what happens if I no longer need God in order to live forever?

WdG: The wager breaks down.

ST: Exactly. God had the monopoly on eternal life for millennia. But no longer. Now you can do business with the Elysium Corporation instead.

WdG: But it's still not as nice as heaven, is it? Doesn't God still have the better offer?

ST: Only if you absolutely believe in Him. Until GM-IM, people wanted to believe in Him because He was the only game in town. But as soon as the corporation came along, the impetus to faith was weaker. There was no need for faith in GM-IM. It was a proven fact. If you had the money, your children could be immortal, or at least they would not age. And living on Elysium gave them an unprecedented opportunity to live forever.

WdG: What if some accident should get you? What if you do die?

ST: My view is that the corporation provides the best chance at immortality. You can call that Trevelyan's Wager.

WdG: But there was nothing your parents could do for themselves.

ST: They still believed in God because they had no other recourse to immortality. I don't blame them.

WdG: How did they live with the contradiction? That they believed in God, but weren't willing to gamble on their daughter?

ST: They just did. People are able to ignore paradox. The need to make sense of the world is that strong.

WdG: So you never brought up the paradox with your parents.

ST: No. I understood it, so there was no need. I'm sure I understood it better than they did. I knew that questions would be difficult for my father in particular.

WdG: Why him?

ST: I'm not sure he was convinced that GM-IM was the best thing for me.

WdG: Why not?

ST: I can't say with certainty, because he kept so much to himself. He kept his thoughts from his own wife, let alone his young daughter. But the impression I got is that my mother and her family prevailed upon him to have the procedure done. I think his resistance may have been religious, as per what we've been discussing. He was very conservative.

WdG: Your mother must have wanted it very badly to win that struggle.

ST: Yes. It's natural enough. Parents want the best for their children, no matter if they're rich or poor.

WdG: Your father died before your mother, correct?

ST: Yes. It was not very difficult for me emotionally, because I was never close to him. He was always distant. Poor man always looked worried, like there was something troubling him. He would never talk about his emotions, so there was no way of knowing what it was. But I remember that his death meant that my mother would die soon. And her death was difficult for me.

WdG: Would you like to talk about it?

ST: I was already graduated and living in my new home on the island. My mother could not come and visit, as a defense against pathogens. We all met our parents in the annexes. When I heard she was very ill, I flew to the annex at Montreal, but then I went to see her at our house in Toronto. She chastised me for it. "Sophia, I told you not to take any risks! I don't even want you going to the annexes!" But inside I think she was pleased I had come to see her. She had many mods herself, but not IM. She was dying of old age.

We talked for a long time. She wasn't in any pain. Not physical, anyway. And she was glad for the chance to talk to me one last time. She told me she was going to heaven to be with her mother and husband. I don't know what happened to the rest of her departed family. Then her eyes went dreamy. But you, Sophia, will be an angel. A living angel here on Earth. I can still hear her voice. You will never know the sadness of seeing your face age in the mirror. You will never see your friends grow old and suffer and die. Every day will be happy. You will be like the nymphs of ancient Greece, your life full of perfect beauty and sublime joy. It will never end, never falter. I daresay that people will even one day pray to you, my little angel. That is my dream for you.

I smiled when she said that. I felt so many things. I felt gratitude to her for the gift of immortal life. I felt like asking her why she denied me eternal life in God's presence, or if she had opposed her husband in that matter, but didn't want to upset her on her deathbed. It was too late, anyway. I was immortal. And I realized that what I was seeing was her own dream. She wanted to be a nymph herself, but time caught up with her. All she could do now was hope that paradise was real. But she took no such risk with me. Her dream would live in me.

WdG: Two hundred pairs of parents had the same dream, it seems.

ST: It's the dream of the ages, from Gilgamesh onward. Ponce de León, Shangri-La, the Taoist alchemists. Even in cultures vastly more religious than ours, people feared death and tried to cheat it. Despite the fact that people will kill over religion, very few of them have absolute faith in it.

WdG: Including Immortals.

ST: Especially Immortals.

WdG: I remember you mentioning the headmaster and the way the parents resisted his moralism. Was it because of his religious streak?

ST: Yes. It was something of a difficult time. The corporation did everything it could to plan ahead. There were some things it didn't foresee.

Originally, we had a chapel house with space for the various religions and denominations. The headmaster was another religious presence here, until we all graduated and he died. But when the initial wave of Immortals graduated and the school closed, so did the chapel. No one wanted it anymore. Well, a handful wanted it to remain. I think the argument was that they needed it to pray for the souls of their ancestors. But after some debate it was decided to close it, and people could pray in their homes if they wanted to.

WdG: Was there much of a conflict over it?

ST: Not too much. Immortals do argue and fight with each other, but they also know they have no alternative to Elysium. We need to get along because there's nowhere else to go. But yes, there is the occasional argument. Sometimes over policy. Privacy versus safety, our relationship with France, things like that. And sometimes over investment strategy. No doubt there will be debates in the future over how many new IMs to permit on Elysium. But, as you will see, there are smaller fights here. Call it friendly competition.

WdG: Over what?

ST: Art, mainly. Musicians and painters competing with each other for the best reviews. If one Immortal criticizes another's work, that could start a vendetta lasting, potentially, forever.

WdG: Have you ever mixed it up with anyone over your architecture?

ST: Someone here wrote a review of my Louvre design and called it too traditional. 'Aesthetically ossified' was the exact phrase. I didn't get into an exchange with him in the print or comment on his films. It wasn't worth it.

WdG: Are Immortals upset if their work is criticized by mortals?

ST: Surprisingly, many are. Many of them seek approval from the outside world. Perhaps it's because the audience here is so limited. Other people think it's silly. The Immortals are the most discriminating audience in the world, and if they like your work, you have permanent appreciation. Undying respect, you could say. So why should we seek the approval of mortals? Some say it's a sign of lack of confidence, aiming too low to be sure of success. Of course mortals will appreciate it. Immortals have infinite time to develop their skills, and there is no way a mortal could match us.

WdG: But the mortals do criticize.

ST: Sure. You put that down to jealousy, or simply a lack of sophistication. It's beyond them, some will say. But I think this sort of thing will become clearer to you after tomorrow night.

Chapter 8

THE INTERVIEWS WERE GOING WELL, or at least easily. Sophia had an outstanding genetically-modified memory. Unlike many interviewees, she was actually answering my questions, rather than trying to steer the conversation to what she wanted to say. Interviews are always negotiations of the truth – the interviewer is hopefully after the most honest version of the truth possible, while the subject generally wants to grind an axe, make themselves appear sympathetic, or both. Between the often-conflicting efforts of the two parties, some version of the truth comes out, and if the interviewer has been good and patient, then the version is fairly objective.

There were problems. There was no way for me to verify most of what Sophia said about life on Elysium. Without the ability to interview other Immortals, I couldn't get another angle. I doubted the servants would say anything, and I knew the Aegis would keep quiet. The only thing I could do was examine what she said logically.

And there was a logical problem. Sophia represented IMs as completely satisfied. If that was so, why did she want to see combat? If Elysium was about risk-management, why willingly go where things were the most dangerous? Was she bored with paradise?

I hadn't pushed yet. Pointing out contradictions or digging for information has to be done slowly in oral histories, and particularly slowly with a person of a certain standing. As a journalist with only a minute to get an interview, I could ask a pointed question to someone I'd never see again. But oral histories take a long time, and earning trust is a big part of them. Sophia seemed completely honest, but the inconsistencies were there, and interviewees usually don't want to hear about them. I hoped to stay long enough for her to become comfortable with me, to trust me enough that I could get to the difficult questions and address the contradictions. It would take a while, but why should I mind, given my present circumstances? The only thing I found irksome was the constant attention of the servants, which jabbed at my populist sensitivities. But this wasn't my world.

I said the interviews were going easily. In a way they were. In another way, it may have been the most difficult project I had ever taken. If it was true that IMs had a completely different worldview from mortals, then I was trying to understand a singular way of thinking different from anything I had ever encountered, even in the most remote regions of the Third World.

The next evening, Sophia offered to take me to an ad-hoc theatre in the town. She told me that, in good weather, outdoor venues were preferred to the town's indoor theater despite the better acoustics there. She said there would be both poetry and music.

Her driver took us down the hill at sunset. I wore the best clothes I'd brought, the same I wore when giving lectures, as I was sometimes hired to do. Sophia wore a black off-the-shoulder dress with lacey sleeves, embroidered with silver thread. I tried not to stare, although back in my world she would have drawn a crowd.

At the town center was the square of smooth cobblestone, flanked by statues and wisterias, with the fountain at the end.

An impromptu restaurant had been erected in the square, with tables and chairs of wrought iron and teak, and velvet loveseats around the perimeter. At the far end of the square from the fountain, a sheer rock face rose up fifty feet, covered in jasmine vine. It provided the backdrop for the stage, which was a circular dais of marble encircled by candelabras. Ornate brass lanterns with colored lenses hung on stands around the square, and each table had candles of its own. There were only a dozen people seated so far.

I followed Sophia to a table. She stood next to her chair, and when I made to pull it out for her, she stopped me with a minute gesture and a servant immediately assisted her.

More servants quickly arrived with silver platters of appetizers, gold-rimmed china, and the ubiquitous chopsticks. I chose Châteauneuf-du-Pape for myself, and as I predicted she abstained from alcohol. She touched the candelabra and the tapers ignited.

"Lovely evening," I said.

"An orchestra will perform later," she said. "Tyler Blendroe puts together groups for occasions like this. And Thomas Allyn will recite poetry."

"How often do you have gatherings like this?" I asked.

"Maybe twice a week," she said. "And many informal gatherings. Impromptu parties and private dinners. But we like to plan an event we can look forward to."

I sipped the wine slowly and looked around at the other Immortals arriving and taking tables or loveseats. They were in pairs or trios, their outfits slightly different from what I saw in London or Rome. They seemed to be blends of old styles and new, but always tasteful and spotless. They all appeared youthful and extremely attractive. They talked and laughed together, but no one came near us. I was brought *tono scottato* with risotto, the tuna cut small to make it easier to eat with chopsticks, and Sophia had minced tarragon lobster. I was distracted from my meal by the lovely surroundings, the Immortals, and Sophia herself. It was all too much.

Fortunately, I finished eating before the evening's entertainment, so it would be easier to give at least that my full attention. The small orchestra assembled at the base of the dais and, without introduction, began to play. It was odd to see someone who appeared so young conducting a group, but conductor and orchestra were both outstanding. They started with Rachmaninoff.

"Do you play in these?" I asked Sophia.

"Occasionally."

The orchestra continued with compositions I didn't recognize. I thought perhaps they were originals, but didn't care to ask Sophia. Even if you have an agreement with someone, they tend to get tired of answering questions after a while, and you have to know when to shut up. Or maybe I wasn't in the mood to pry anymore, as the sun went down and the stars appeared overhead, and a warm breeze gently fluttered the candle flames. The lanterns came on and fireflies appeared. It seemed the musicians had planned their repertoire to match the changing light of sunset, the mood wandering from bright to sublime, complimenting the atmosphere of the square like wine expertly paired with food. Perhaps they improvised their set to match the evening. Or perhaps it was just me.

When the sky glow was nearly faded, Allyn took the dais, dressed somewhat as a courtier of Henry the Eighth and illuminated by soft lantern light. The orchestra played very softly behind him as he spoke — not that they needed such care, as his voice was very powerful. I doubt I'd ever heard an unamplified voice so strong. He started with a few poems unfamiliar to me. The orchestra played short interludes between his stanzas.

Finally, he recited the lines from Marlowe which I remembered from a mentor's bookshelf, many years before:

I hold the Fates bound fast in iron chains,
And with my hand turn Fortune's wheel about;
And sooner shall the sun fall from his sphere
Then I be slain or overcome.
Draw forth thy sword, thou mighty man-at-arms,
Intending but to raze my charmed skin,
And Jove himself will stretch his hand from heaven
To ward the blow, and shield me safe from harm.
See, how he rains down heaps of gold in showers,
As if he meant to give my soldiers pay!
We will reign as consuls of the earth,
And mighty kings shall be our senators.
Jove sometime masked in a shepherd's weed;
by those steps that he hath scaled the heavens
May we become immortal like the gods.

The orchestra struck up a Wagnerian tone at the conclusion of his recitation, but it quickly and seamlessly moved into something much more subtle — Debussy, I think. They finished with a stately movement I had never heard.

The musicians stood and bowed to receive the applause of their fellow Immortals. Their servants packed the instruments while they took tables for their own meals.

"That was amazing," I said.

"Tyler usually comes up with something good," said Sophia.

She continued eating in silence while I sipped my wine and looked around. There were many couples present, men with their arms around women who had shawls around their shoulders in the evening breeze.

"Are you getting cold?" I asked. She didn't have a shawl.

"I thought we might go somewhere," she said. "I have a café in mind I think you'll like."

"Okay," I said.

We walked along the cheerfully-lit main street, where only a handful of people were visible, and turned down a narrow alley paved with cobblestones. The walls were covered in ivy, and colored lanterns lit our way. There was a small courtyard with a black marble fountain. The window boxes were full of flowers in the moonlight.

We passed through a tunnel, a low barrel vault just higher than my head, and into another courtyard surrounded by an arcade with marble columns. There was another fountain in the center, and windows of stained glass under the arcade. They must have modeled the place after a monastery in Spain or Italy. The Milky Way was distinct overhead.

We sat at a table by the fountain. It was warmer here, although I couldn't see any manner of heating. Servants quickly appeared. I asked for Fundador and Sophia surprised me by ordering schnapps.

"Rare occasion," she said.

"Think anyone else went out for drinks?"

"Maybe. Maybe they'll stay and talk until the sun comes up and breakfast is brought to them. Maybe go down to the surf and make love and sleep there. Maybe just go home. But no one will come here."

"Why not?"

"We're here."

"I noticed none of the Immortals came to talk to you."

"I've been labeled a rebel for bringing you here," she said.

"I hope I haven't caused you any trouble," I said.

"Oh, it's nothing. Not compared to what they'll call me after you take me into combat."

"I'm mortal, and people tell me that *I'm* crazy."

"They'll probably say I was putting immortality to the test."

The drinks arrived and we touched glasses.

"*A votre santé*," I said. "It seems like a safe bet."

"To your good fortune," she said.

"It's held so far."

"I'd say so."

"Were your compatriots afraid they'd catch a pathogen from me?"

"Hardly. I'm afraid they view you as the pathogen. They don't like mortals here."

"The servants and Aegis are all mortal."

"Under our direction," she said. "We don't control you. You're a free mortal. You're the outside world."

"I'm no threat to them."

"Doesn't matter. They see you as a defilement. This is Elysium, realm of Immortals. To them, you represent the gross world."

"How did you get them to let me in?"

"I based my arguments on legal grounds. Rights to visitors, private property rights, and so on. Brought in a few friends, legal theorists, to argue for me. The corporation ruled that it could not prevent me from bringing you here, as long as you passed the security checks. But a few residents are now trying to pass a regulation against visitors. It may well be that you are the only mortal to ever come here and leave."

"You'll be the first Immortal to see combat," I said. I momentarily tried to imagine her in body armor with a camera and press pass. It was a strain.

"You know, I read your biography," she said. "But I've never found any mention of why you chose to become a war correspondent in the first place."

"I've never been interviewed on the subject."

"Surely you didn't just stumble into it."

"No," I said. "It's not the sort of career you just fall into."

"Have you thought about why you do it?"

"Sure. All the time I've spent sitting around in airports and bus stops, I've thought about it plenty."

"Go ahead."

"I was raised in the Catholic Church, like you were," I said. "Well, not like you. Middle-class. Small-town. In my family, intelligence was useful for school or work, but not really for thinking with. The Church and the family did the thinking. My job as a child was to sit still, shut up, memorize what I was taught, and get good grades. As long as I did that, people would speak nicely to me and tell each other, in front of me, what a good boy I was."

"It sounds like you didn't enjoy it."

"No. They were harsh people, my family and the nuns who taught in the Catholic school. The easiest thing to do was just keep my thoughts to myself and go along."

"And your father?"

"Died when I was six."

"I'm sorry."

"I had two sisters and no brothers," I said. "My mother broke with my father's family after his death, because she never liked them, and that was mutual. On my mother's side of the family, there were only women."

"No uncles?"

"I had one. My grandmother's only son. He was killed in Haiti during one of the interventions. My mother always told me that he was the sweetest, gentlest person she'd ever known, although I knew that he was Special Forces.

"One time, during Thanksgiving dinner, I asked my grandmother why her son had joined the Army. She said that he had been raised in a house full of women, and by nuns in Catholic school, and wanted to know what a man's world was like."

"And your upbringing was the same."

"Exactly. If there was something missing from his life that made him want to go to war, then I had the same deficiency."

"That's why you became a journalist?"

"Part of it," I said. "There were others. Like Ballard. There were some boys in my neighborhood. They were middle-class, but the not the better sort my mother thought our family was.

She tried to keep me away from them, but you can't watch someone all the time. We found some local drunk to buy whiskey for us. We learned where to get weed in our little town."

"Get what?"

"Weed."

"Weeds?"

"Marijuana," I said.

"Oh."

"The weed was good but the cigarettes made me choke. But anyway, one of the boys knew a man named Ballard. Ballard had been a Catholic priest. Billy told me that he'd been defrocked because he was gay. Joe said he'd left voluntarily after the church tried to silence him for things he'd said about his beliefs.

"Joe and I sometimes stopped by the trailer where he lived. He seemed kind of exotic to me. He'd serve us broiled escargot or Turkish coffee. Tell us stories of his travels. I remember one day I was browsing his bookshelf and found *The Antichrist* by Nietzsche. I asked him if I could borrow it, because I figured it was a horror novel. He said, sure you can borrow it. You can borrow whatever you like.

"Ballard's bookshelf became my personal library from my sophomore year of high school. Those few linear feet completely changed my life. Not gently, either. It was like the world exploded around me. I read Marx, Freud, *Origins of the Species*, the *Bhagavad Gita*, all kinds of things. When I brought them back to Ballard, we'd discuss them over coffee. It was clear that he was not a traditional Catholic. I asked him why he'd become a priest, and he told me he thought there was something truly spiritual in people, and that he'd wanted to explore it by becoming a priest. But he said it turned out that he couldn't be an explorer and a priest at the same time.

"Everything was changing for me. In the books, I learned that my mother's beliefs were an elitist imposition meant to control the masses. And every day I learned how shallow my family was. I was experimenting with sex and drugs, and reading atheist philosophy, but since I kept up decent grades and didn't say upsetting things, they all loved me and approved. It was like a play. All I had to do was recite the lines. And I was exploring the dark places in myself and I was changing. I was getting smarter and meaner.

"My last year of high school, I was working at the local news service, just doing manual labor. That was a hard year for me. I hated my family and I hated school. Then I found another kind of book on Ballard's shelf. It was a collection of dispatches from different war correspondents — Steinbeck, Hemingway, and Reese. I read it in one day. War seemed horribly magical to me. Like a monster that chewed up bourgeois illusions and exposed the truth of human life. It seemed like a harsh utopia where everything was made clear. And I remembered what my grandmother had said about her son. Now I understood. He hadn't fought for his country. He'd done it for himself. The Army was just how he chose to see what he wanted to see.

"After reading that book, I knew I wanted to see war. But I wouldn't be a soldier; I'd go as a journalist. For the first time in my life I had a purpose of my own. I threw myself into it. I didn't know I had that kind of energy in me.

"I went down to the reporters' offices to see if anyone would help me. I wanted to go out with them on the weekends and help them cover their beats. I had a little experience from the high school news club. None of them wanted me around except the youngest one, John Rhodes. He took me with him to city council meetings and accident scenes. I learned about politics, legal procedure, police work. I did some of the shooting and helped him write copy. I graduated from high school. That was a non-event for me except for the time it freed up.

"Then I got a freelance position with the service and was writing under my own byline. I wrote an investigative story on gang violence among migrant workers in the town. People wrote the editor to say they had no idea such things went on in our little town."

"What did your family think?" she asked.

"They weren't sure what to make of it. They were happy that I had a career with the news service. My family was blue-collar and didn't care what kind of job I had, so long as I had one. It didn't matter to them if I went to college or not. But they didn't like this dabbling in darkness. My mom realized that I had mingled with criminals in order to write the story. But she couldn't say anything, because other people told her they liked my work."

"Did your mother know that you wanted to be a war correspondent?"

"No. She wouldn't have approved, so I didn't say anything. But John approved. He told me I should keep looking at the dark side of life, because that's where all the good stuff is.

"But for the first time in my life, I felt confident. I knew I was more streetwise than my readers, and more intelligent and educated than the punks I'd written about. My mother's bourgeois values were laughable. I had an edge on me, like a controlled acceptance of my own evil. And I had a dream and a plan and my youth. I felt great.

"I still had a long way to go. I didn't have any international experience, and my Spanish from high school wasn't fluent. I knew I'd need the Spanish. Then I could work in Latin America, with the new wave of climate wars that was starting, and the Spanish would give me access to most every country except Brazil. And I knew I'd have to freelance. I didn't have any college, so I couldn't get a position with a big news service. I'd have to go down there and get the stories and shop them around. And if I could cover something where there were no other journalists, they'd almost have to take my stories.

"I told my family I was going to look for work in New York. I did go to New York, but then got on a plane for Mexico City. I traveled around Mexico for a couple of months, working on my Spanish. I found a local student who paid me a little money for English lessons."

"How old were you at that point?" asked Sophia.

"I guess I was twenty," I said. "That's right, I turned twenty-one down there. I was young. It was my first time out of the country. It was my first time living alone."

"Were you scared?"

"I guess I was. I felt a lot of things. Nervous, excited, confused, curious, determined...I knew that this was the turning point in my life. I had to get my Spanish down and go get a story."

"But was there a revolt in Mexico at the time?"

"Nothing violent at the time. You know, it would boil up now and then. But after two months of working and traveling, I met a guy in Puebla who was going to drive down to Guatemala. I told him I'd split the gas with him and I caught a ride.

"It wasn't far into Guatemala that we decided to head for a small town a few miles off the Pan-American Highway. There was a Mayan ruin we wanted to see. When we got to the town, we ran into a roadblock. There were guys with guns, with bandanas over their faces. They said the town was closed off and that we had to go. I asked what was happening, and they said that they'd kicked out the mayor and the city council and seized control of the town. It had happened only an hour before, and the state police hadn't even made it out there yet.

"So I told them I was a journalist. Took out my pass from the Associated Press. Fake as a rubber check, but I figured I'd need one, so I'd made it in New York. I told them I'd get their story out to the world. They let me in. The guy I was riding with went back the way we came and I stayed. They took me to their *comandante*, who was suspicious but also realized that I could be useful. They needed to get their side of the situation out, and if the government censored the in-country media, which it would, then I was their best shot.

"He explained that, the day before, someone from the government had come by with a couple of policemen for extra weight. He went house-to-house, telling everyone that they could no longer go to the river for their water. And that they had to take down their rainwater catch basins. The government had signed a contract with a French company to provide water for the village. The company would bring water in a truck every Friday, and each family would pay a water tax and take their water. But collecting water themselves was a violation of the contract, and therefore a crime."

"I can guess why the government signed the contract," said Sophia.

"They said it was to prevent waterborne disease. But the people didn't believe it. They always boiled the water first anyway. And they knew the rainwater was clean. The government took a kickback from the company.

"So when the suit and his cops left, the people went to the mayor. He said he'd approved the contract because it was good for the community. He got his cut.

"So the people went home and, first thing in the morning, they all came back with guns. They captured the mayor, the two cops, and the city council, and sent them all down the road. Then they dug foxholes around the town and waited for the police."

"Isn't that a somewhat strong reaction?"

"If you have recourse to the law, yes. So in Guatemala, no."

"Then what happened?"

"They were still fortifying the place when I got there. I quickly wrote up the story, got the photos, and planned on leaving first thing in the morning. I couldn't send it from the town because the satellite phone wasn't working and we were way off the Net. I'd have to go back to the highway and catch a bus to the nearest city. They hoped the UN and the international NGOs would pressure the government before anything violent happened.

"The army beat me to the punch. They surrounded the town at first light and I couldn't get out. The townspeople didn't get the chance to negotiate. They told the army not to approach within a hundred meters of the town, which it did, probably to prove who was in charge. The townspeople opened fire and suddenly everyone was running and shouting, and I couldn't tell what was happening.

"The townspeople were not very well armed, but they had done well to dig themselves in. The army didn't have any heavy weapons, so they couldn't break into the town. The people only had some hunting rifles, plus the guns they took from the police station. The mayor was a skeet shooting champion, so the people took his gun from his house, and the local drug dealer had a pretty nice gun himself.

"I got some good footage of the fighting, or at least of the townspeople fighting. I never could see any of the soldiers. They just sprayed the town down with bullets, then tried to enter. The townspeople held their fire until they had a good shot. They had to because they didn't have much ammunition. And they were hunters, so they were pretty good shots. And then they got the idea to only shoot for the legs. That way, you take out two men with one bullet — the man you shot, and another man to carry him out.

"Two of the townsmen were killed and two were wounded. The wounded stayed in their positions and I got shots of the dead. They were the first corpses I'd seen outside of a casket. I was surprised how much blood comes out of a person. But the army didn't press home the attack.

"The *comandante*, who was really just a rancher and former soldier, wasn't happy. He wanted to negotiate a solution because he knew it was the only way out. But when the shooting started, he thought they were finished. All they have to do is bring up a tank, he told me, and we're all dead. We're fifty kilometers off the Pan-American Highway, how long could it possibly take?

"I told him I'd sneak through the army's line at night and get the story out. If the world knew, it might prevent a massacre. All he had to do was open negotiations with the army — tell them we have women and children here. Keep them talking until I got the story out. So he sent a young guy with me as a guide. Guy named Carlos. He'd take me up the hill at the back of the town. There was a goat path up the hill the soldiers wouldn't be watching. We'd walk six miles to the next village, and the *comandante's* friend there would drive us into the city. If we left just after dark, we'd be in the city before sunrise, and the story would be all over the Net by noon.

"So Carlos and I went up the hill just after sunset. We couldn't bring flashlights because we'd be spotted. Carlos knew the way in the dark and he could walk fast. The path looked like a thin grey ribbon in the dark. When the moon was behind the clouds, it was pitch black, and I just walked towards the sound of Carlos' footsteps.

"We got to a narrow pass at the summit, and the army had a couple of guys guarding the trail. There was no way around them, with a steep rise on either side, unless we tried to pick our way through the jungle in the dark, which would make a lot of noise and take all night, if I made it at all. The soldiers were sitting by a fire about twenty feet from the trail. We decided the only thing to do was sneak as close as possible and then make a break for it. We'd wait for the moon to go behind a cloud. I wasn't happy with trying to run on the trail in the dark. I thought I'd trip and get shot. But I just lay there watching a cloud slowly slip across the moon.

"When Carlos bolted, I was right behind him. Lucky for us, it wasn't far around a bend in the path that put a boulder between us and them. We barreled down that trail in the dark with the bullets ricocheting off the rocks. It was one of the few times anyone has shot at me specifically. I couldn't see anything except the moonlit clouds through a break in the trees — that's how I knew where the trail was. They must've had night vision gear, so I'm surprised we didn't get shot.

"At the bottom of the hill, we hit the road to the next town. Carlos wanted to keep running, but I couldn't. I wasn't used to the altitude. But when we saw that no one was behind us, we started laughing about the whole thing. Those soldiers must've been surprised as hell at two crazy *muchachos* running right past them in the dark. Now those fools have to report that two guys got past them, and they'll get reprimanded. We laughed at the poor chastised soldiers, and I thought about them radioing in the incident, and I told Carlos we should run again.

"So the *comandante's* friend gave us a lift in his pickup to the city. He gave us beers and laughed all the way at the story of the crazy *muchachos* running right past the soldiers. He made us tell him the story three times.

"I got the story out to Associated Press as soon as we had access. I wasn't even out of the truck yet. They had to take the story because I had good combat footage. It was just too sexy to refuse. Not to mention there was a big OAS conference coming up, and Guatemala was supposed to chair the human

rights roundtable. The story was out in hours. There was even
a little footage of Carlos. He just couldn't believe it. There he
was with his rifle, fighting the army for all the world to see. I
printed some still frames of him from the footage and gave
them to him. I'll bet he still has them on the wall in his house.

"We ate at a restaurant that one of Carlos' uncles owned
— Carlos told him the story of the *muchachos locos* — and
washed up a bit in the kitchen. Then the three of us drove back
to an overlook with a good view of the village. I shot some
footage of the army cordon and could see the *comandante* and
an officer in negotiations. The story must have set off a
firestorm, because a few hours later the governor drives up in a
caravan of luxury cars with several journalists. We climbed
down and showed up just in time to record the governor
declaring that the water contract was being voided and that the
army was leaving. The *comandante*, I think, would've liked to see
a few people held accountable, but decided not to push his
luck for something he knew he wouldn't have gotten anyway.

"That night there was an impromptu fiesta in the *zocalo* in
front of the little church. Everyone was congratulating Carlos
and I and saying that the *comandante* would be the new mayor.
The dead were in the church, wrapped in bedsheets at the altar,
and all night long people were going in to light candles and
pray for them before going back out to the fiesta to drink more
Gallo. The wounded were taken to the hospital and the dead
would have to be buried the next day. But everyone was happy
that the army they hated so much had been beaten. I
remember, plain as day, how I felt sitting in front of the
bonfire in the *zocalo* with everyone. I'd done it. I'd been under
fire, gotten the story, and published under my own byline on

the Net, worldwide. Associated Press paid me and sent me a real press pass. I was a war correspondent. And the voyage of growing up, that started with Ballard's bookshelf, was over."

I sat in silence and sipped the Fundador, my mind back in Guatemala, with the faces in the firelight and Carlos laughing and the blood-stained white sheets in the church. Then I noticed the silence and looked up. Sophia was watching me intensely and her face was flush.

"I can't believe you did that," she said.

"Did what?"

"Risked your life like that. And so young, too!"

"I had to," I said.

"No you didn't."

"I know."

"The men here would never do something like that. They're not brave at all."

"Rourke was brave going into that club," I said.

"No," she laughed. "Rourke was ignorant. I'll bet he hasn't left the annexes after that night. Immortal men aren't brave, because they don't want to risk their lives. Only mortals will do that."

As I held her eyes, I knew everything about my visit to Elysium had changed — the project, my relationship with Sophia, and my reason for staying there.

Chapter 9

I WOKE IN THE MORNING with the Mediterranean breeze
billowing the curtains, and I could tell from the light it was
very early. The room was high and airy, with potted hibiscus
and bougainvilleas throughout. The flowers seemed an
extension of the garden beyond the glass wall, so it was hard to
tell if we were indoors or out.

Sophia lay next to me in bed, facing away. She had the
softest skin of any woman I'd met, without the slightest
blemish, mark, or mole anywhere on her.

I'd rolled out the war stories many times before to get
what I wanted. I don't know if I'd done it intentionally the
night before. Maybe it was just habit. Generally I told the
stories truly, because the truth was more compelling than what
I could invent. I left things out, though. I left out how I'd
become inured to peoples' suffering, and of how I used the
people I met, just as they used me. I left out the darkest parts
of the stories. I was never able to forget I was doing so.

"What are you thinking about?" asked Sophia. I hadn't
realized she was awake.

"War stories," I said.

"You have good ones."

They get the job done, I thought.

She rose and I watched her walk to the shower. There was
no curtain or stall, just the brass knobs surrounded by Italian
tiling. She didn't look at me as I watched her shower. Her
movements were unhurried. I had a subtle and slightly
disturbing sense that she was unreal, like some kind of image

or projection. After she dried herself, she put on a satin robe similar to a kimono. She came over to the bed, wordlessly took my hand, and led me across the room to a cedar chest. From the chest she took a deep blue silk robe in the Japanese style, embroidered with gold and scented with jasmine, which she tied around me.

We went out onto a teak deck overlooking a wide field, still heavy with dew, with an old apple tree in the middle. As we sat at the table, the servants, as always, came in like actors appearing on stage with café au lait, croissants, kippers and eggs, and pâté on fresh bread. And now I was feeling a little rebellious.

One of the servants was a young Latina with whom I made eye contact.

"Thank you," I said with a smile. Maybe I could be a bad influence here.

"Yes, sir," she said, quickly looking away.

"Hungry?" asked Sophia.

"Very."

We ate in silence.

"You're concerned," she said.

"Yeah."

"I'm sure you've ended up in this situation in the past."

"Sometimes."

"How have you handled it?"

"Case-by-case, I guess. It's never part of the plan." I wondered if I was lying.

"I shouldn't think so. But you won't have any problems with me."

"Thanks. I don't think you'll have a problem with me."

"I know I won't. I can see I won't."

"Then you know more about me than I do."

"Women's intuition?"

"Is there a mod for that?"

"No. But you shouldn't be surprised if someone can see things about you that you don't."

"You don't worry about your reputation?"

"No," she laughed. "They already think poorly of me. Not that the servants would say anything."

"Do the Immortals get into relationships with the servants?"

"Wouldn't surprise me if they sleep with them from time to time, just on a whim. Not the Aegis, though. They won't do it. And no one would go beyond just a tryst with a servant. But I imagine that people do it out of boredom."

"How do you get bored here?"

"Well...for one thing, we're all very well educated. Our tastes are highly refined. So it's easy for us to be critical, and reject everything. The shows in the square, like last night, are usually good. But we've all heard so much great music, for at least a hundred years, that we become jaded. It's the same with all the arts.

"Take Tariq. He lives down close to the village. Wonderful pianist, but very critical and aggressive. Doesn't like anyone's work, not even his own, really. He's pushed himself hard from the very beginning to be the greatest pianist in history. He's outstanding, but honestly, I've always found him insufferable. Good Lord, the way he and Sarah Pratchet fight. He needs everyone to know he's better than her. They are both so good that not even IMs can tell who is better. They play competitions against each other, like fighting duels. Playing the most complicated pieces they can find or write, at breakneck speed. Then argue about who had won. If you didn't think Tariq did, it was only because you lacked the subtlety to appreciate his technique, you see.

"Even the few things he likes can't satisfy him. One time, after a show in the village, he told me it was all like a sunset. If you see a beautiful sunset, you can only enjoy it for a little while, because the sun sets and it's over. But our sun never sets, he said. You'll always have these beautiful things to enjoy. That weakens them. They would be more beautiful if they didn't last."

"Do you think he had a point?"

"Yes, but a moot one," she said. "It's still better to be immortal. Is the sunset so beautiful that you would die for it? No. We may not view the world as beautifully as a mortal does, but we view it forever. The world is only so poignant to a mortal because of his inexperience."

We finished breakfast and I went inside and showered. I wondered why the Immortals would think something like bedding a servant would satisfy them, if the best music in the world couldn't. Just the novelty of it? It seemed cruel and desperate and small. And then I stopped thinking about it, because I suddenly felt like I understood it a bit too well.

Chapter 10

I LOST TRACK of how much time I'd spent on Elysium, the way you forget the date when you're on a long vacation. Sophia and I spent every day together. We swam in the harbor, or naked in the surf south of the village. We both got quite dark from the sun, although her skin remained very soft. We rode her horses in the early morning sun up the hill and through the forest in the interior of the island, and brought our own food without servants to accompany us. We'd make love in the forests and fields with only the horses to see us, and sleep under the stars wrapped in a blanket. We spent a few days at sea in her sailboat, visiting the small, uninhabited islands nearby, and attended more concerts in the village, although the other Immortals continued to avoid us. Every night we slept together and every day there was the perfect weather and fine food. I did a few more interviews with her, mostly to keep up the pretense that I was still working. She talked about her early education, and the riding and fencing competitions when she was a teenager, about her little adventures with childhood friends in Paris or Siena, and the first time she was drunk, and how she got her contacts in the world of architecture. I told her war stories, of how people behaved when laws and norms collapsed and the things they kept suppressed came out. She listened very closely to the stories about a world so different from her own, perhaps in part to prepare herself for visiting it.

One afternoon we were sitting on the beach after swimming. A huge three-masted sailing ship, over eighty meters long, came into the harbor escorted by a small Aegis patrol boat.

"Nice ship," I said.

"Young-Il Chen's," said Sophia.

"It does look a bit junk-like. National pride?"

"Every kind of pride."

"Ever been out on it?"

"Sure. She throws parties on it. And we made some trips on it when we worked together."

"What work was that?"

"She had the brilliant idea of running a development NGO in West Africa. Trying to jump start the economies in the most densely-populated areas. She roped a few Immortals into her plan, including yours truly.

"So we anchored that ship off the coast of Liberia, surrounded by security. Young-Il's plan looked good on paper: simultaneously increase education, manufacturing, and communication and transportation infrastructure. We'd clear all the bottlenecks at once and the money would flow.

"It started off well enough. We had well-publicized meetings with African leaders aboard the ship, and even went ashore a couple of times. The Aegis weren't too happy about that, but no one got hurt. The media loved it because IMs were involved. So we were headline news for a while."

"How did it work out?" I asked.

"Comedy of errors. Naturally, it all looked good in the press. But the governments we were dealing with were unbelievably corrupt. We were appalled at the greed. Every penny they could embezzle, they took. It wasn't hard to do; the politicians owned the banks that received the development funds. The construction contracts went to their own companies or else their cronies. They stole what they could, and rarely finished any of the projects. At one point, in Senegal, we diverted money to farms because there was a drought, and famine looked possible. But the president directed the funds to his own farms, for seed and new machinery, and instead of food grew cash crops, which he sold abroad and pocketed the money."

"Did you realize what was happening?" I asked.

"Sure we realized it. We had agents on the ground reporting to us. The governments delayed, lied, made excuses, promises, whatever they could do to keep the money coming. We tried to get them to cooperate, but we only had so much power. We tried to work through people lower in the bureaucracies, who were actually doing the work, but they were all corrupt, too. For months we tried to make it work. Young-Il was getting more and more frustrated at the whole thing. Every time we tried, we found ourselves robbed by a band of thieves.

"Finally we had a meeting one evening and we decided we had to stop. Some of our mortal consultants insisted that we had made some progress by changing tactics. By switching to microloans to small businesses, we were getting the money straight to the people instead of the government. If we could strengthen the *petite bourgeoisie* that way, we might even help the development of democratic institutions.

"Young-Il didn't like the idea. It would take forever, she said. She wanted one unified plan that would remake the economy of West Africa in ten years. She thought she could just engineer the system however she wanted, through money and politics. But it ended up being much more complicated than she thought. When it didn't go as planned, she got angry. It was the mortals' fault, not hers. So we weighed anchor and left. I was happy it was over. I was tired of the whole silly thing."

"What happened to the projects you started?"

"I don't know. I don't care, either. It's their problem, not mine."

That night I lay awake in bed, watching the moon through the skylight while Sophia slept next to me. The story she'd told me about the development project had reminded me of something, but I couldn't remember what it was. It was like an itch in my mind, and it was still there when I went to sleep. Then I woke in the middle of the night and I remembered. It was the story I hadn't told Sophia, the story of what happened in El Salvador before I met Lucia on the flight out. I played it over and over in my head. Something Emilio had said years ago, and I just now understood it. And I regretted that I didn't understand before, because now Emilio was dead and I couldn't thank him.

I told Sophia the story the next day. Parts of it horrified her and others made no impression. Interesting story, she said without enthusiasm. Since the night I remembered the story, everything changed for me, but we didn't discuss it. She must have known it was true. She could tell from the silences, or how my curiosity waned, or how things were in bed, which is a bad place to try to hide what you feel.

Sophia had taught me something of great value although she wasn't trying. She could enjoy exquisite luxuries with her health and youth intact, in a beautiful place with beautiful people, theoretically, forever. And she wasn't satisfied. Wasn't she always looking for the next distraction? Wasn't that what I was to her? I had spent my life trying to satisfy my desires, just as she had. I'd been living as if I'd never die, bouncing from one desire to the next. Sophia was doing the same, but for her it made much more sense. She had tremendous advantages over me. If she couldn't find satisfaction in pleasure, it was virtually impossible for me. If it was a lost cause, why continue trying?

To this point I would have answered that there was no alternative. Then I remembered what Emilio had said. Now I thought maybe there was a way out of the impossible situation of human life, a way that didn't depend on constantly fighting the world to make it give me what I wanted. I saw I needn't envy anyone. The Immortals could be brilliant, but they couldn't be great, not the way Emilio was great. Since the sunset is only temporary, Sophia lived for the one thing she thought was eternal, which was herself. Emilio wouldn't live or die for the sunset, or even for himself, but he had something else, and that opened the door for him. The Immortals' security, their victory over life and death, strangled all their motivation for greatness and they gambled away what Emilio had found. Trevelyan's Wager had broken down.

I couldn't stay on Elysium after that. I told Sophia I had to go get things done back in the world, which was true. I thanked her for her generosity and promised to repay her by taking her with me on my next field assignment. She seemed bored by that prospect, thank God. Perhaps she'd had enough of war stories and story-tellers, and would shortly be on to the next thing. The look in her eyes had certainly changed. And I'm sure she won't speak to me again after I publish this. But I was profoundly relieved that I didn't need to take Sophia into a war zone and, most likely, get her killed. I'd dodged quite a few bullets in my life, but maybe that was the biggest.

I got back on the little aircraft that had carried me to Elysium, and returned to Marseille, where the noise and pollution came as a shock. Then I took the train to Paris and began transcribing the interviews. I worked nonstop to get the story down. *Pas de temps à perdre,* no time to lose.

I will end with the story of the Salvadoran lawyer whose death changed my life as I remembered it one night on Elysium, lying next to a sleeping nymph who, eternally young, will continue to seek her happiness on that sunny island long after I am forgotten.

* * *

During that last trip to El Salvador, I interviewed a human rights lawyer named Emilio. He was working on behalf of the poor of San Salvador during the revolt, when the government death squads were intimidating and killing anyone suspected of disloyalty. The death squads were all former soldiers or off-duty police, but the government wanted deniability and claimed it knew nothing about them. Emilio constantly lodged legal protests with the government. The judiciary was firmly in the executive's pocket, but Emilio's lawsuits on behalf of the people made news on the Net. Sometimes the government acquiesced to save a little political capital, but that only made Emilio more famous, and therefore more powerful.

I met him just before noon one March day on the steps of the courthouse as he came out from appealing a verdict. I had called him a few days before, so he was expecting me. He was no one you would notice in a crowd. He was rather tall and very thin, with wavy black hair and a thick moustache. He was quiet, but friendly and polite. I had asked for an interview, and he invited me to accompany him to his next appointment. We took a taxi to an outdoor café where he was meeting with activists he'd been representing. They bought him lunch and let me listen to the debriefing so I could file the report. The activists deeply respected him and thanked him for his work. Then he said he had to meet more clients on the other side of town and asked me to come along. I accepted, and his clients gave us a lift in an old car to an abandoned factory another NGO was using.

That group was running an orphanage for children abandoned in the war, feeding and educating them as well as they could. The place was full of peeling paint, empty metal window frames, bright plastic buckets in closets for toilets, and hundreds of children. The children were dressed in cast-offs from the developed world, faded and patched, with logos of TV shows or rock bands or products they would never buy. Their laughter and crying echoed through the wide corridors. All those tiny, dirty bare feet on the concrete floor.

The caretakers told Emilio the police had been threatening to shut them down unless they paid the appropriate bribes for doing business in this neighborhood, which they couldn't. Emilio told them he'd file an injunction with the courts to prevent the closure, but that they would need to reach out to other NGOs, maybe international ones, to generate enough attention to keep the police at bay.

"You should take some pictures here," he told me. "The media likes pictures of cute little children, doesn't it?" I took the pictures and filed them with the service to help him out. And yes, the media likes pictures of cute little children.

Emilio gave them a list of contacts with national NGOs and asked about the police threats. They gave him the information while changing diapers and wiping noses. He said they'd hear from him in about two weeks about the injunction, but gave them his number so they could contact him if any emergency arose. They listened closely and thanked him for his time.

He said he had another appointment to keep and that I could come if I wanted. He led me on foot through the streets and into a packed outdoor market shaded by plastic tarps overhead. He wove through the maze of stalls full of vegetables, meat, and flowers and spices I didn't recognize, and three or four people stopped him to ask how he was and to thank him for what he'd done for them. He seemed to be taking us on a zigzagging course through the market; I noticed he kept looking behind him, and not for me. We exited onto the streets through the back of a cantina with Emilio's nod to the bartender.

We arrived at the home of a local activist for a meeting; the courtyard behind the house sported barbed wire atop the adobe walls, and was filled with about a hundred people at plastic tables and chairs. They had formed a sort of mutual assistance co-op to keep each other in food, make sure the children were cared for, and help each other with medical bills. The government was suspicious of them because it thought they were helping the insurgents. They wanted to create a formal NGO to gain some legal protections. Emilio lectured for about two hours on what the process entailed, what paperwork they needed to submit, and so on, all off the top of his head. They took notes, and he helped them form into committees and delegate tasks. He told them how to work with the local media and make connections with the national NGOs, and about where they might get grants. They gave him a little food as he answered questions, and a bundle of chicken tamales wrapped in banana leaves as we left. It was dusk now.

"Where are you staying tonight, *joven?*" he asked.

"I haven't gotten a hotel room in town yet. I just came in this morning."

"Well, you might as well come with me. You can do an interview if you want."

"I probably wouldn't be able to get a hotel room at this hour," I said.

"And we shouldn't be out at night anyway."

"No, we shouldn't."

I followed him to the home of another family he was staying with for a few days. Their oldest son had been picked up by the army at a checkpoint and accused of sedition, but Emilio had gotten him released. We all ate together in the tiny dining room, and Emilio shared the tamales with them. He talked with them about local matters, the police, and the corrupt city council while we drank their Pilsener, and they asked me if I thought the United States would send troops to fight the insurgency. They offered Emilio and me their bedroom, but Emilio insisted we'd sleep on the floor in the parlor. Anyway, we still have some work to do, he told them. They went to sleep and Emilio worked at the kitchen table on his old computer, filling out forms for a court challenge. I wrote up a story about what I'd seen that day, with the pictures of the cute children, and sent it off to the service. When I fell asleep on the couch, Emilio was still working. That was the first day I spent with him.

I stayed with him for two weeks. Every day was the same routine – above fourteen hours of work, staying with friends because he didn't charge for his services and couldn't afford rent. Someone told me the government periodically froze his bank accounts, so money did him no good anyway. He never complained about anything, but he did always sit facing the door.

I told myself I was getting outstanding stories by staying with him. Associated Press tired of them quickly, but I sold them to other outlets. I told myself it was good for my career, which it wasn't, and that I was keeping Emilio alive, because the government didn't want to kill him with a foreign journalist around to see it. That was true, but the real reason I was there was that he fascinated me. He had no wife, children, home, or money. Just the people he worked with, all day, every day.

I asked him why he kept doing it, and he said his work was his real food. If he saw people being hurt, he couldn't be happy, so he had to help them. And then they helped him in return because they wanted to. His work wasn't romantic, or even, fundamentally, political. It was personal. As I watched it happening, I could see that something new was being created every day. But you don't have to work as hard as you do, I said. He said that he didn't have much time on this earth and that he wanted to do all he could with what he had left. *No hay tiempo que perder*, no time to lose. No sense in wasting time with things that don't matter. He couldn't count on having even the next day. There was nothing complicated about it, and I understood it intellectually, but I was looking at it from the outside and couldn't understand him. I just wrote down what he said.

Then there was a government offensive along the coast and the news service wanted me to get footage and write some copy. So I told Emilio I had to head south for a few days, but that I'd be back soon. He said, sure, *joven*, go, I'll see you when you get back. I didn't want to leave because I was afraid of what might happen. I don't know what I was hoping for. I couldn't stay there forever.

When I got back he was dead. The people had already buried him in the churchyard of a nearby village. They told me the story of what had happened.

He had gone to the village, as he often did, to work with the *campesinos*. A death squad came one night while he was there. Maybe they'd been watching to see if I was with him. They gathered everyone in the village into the square to make them watch. The ancient, simple-minded delusion: if we just get tougher, harsher, all the problems will go away. We'll beat the world into submission. It has never worked and it never will work.

They held everyone, even the little children, at gunpoint as they brought Emilio out. The men couldn't do anything with guns pointed at their families except watch.

The soldiers hacked Emilio with machetes like butchering an animal. The women and children wailed as they watched the man they loved being slaughtered and the men cried tears of rage. All the men told me they were joining the insurgents to avenge his death. They didn't care if they died. They wouldn't live in a world where things like that happened.

Before they killed him, the soldiers dragged Emilio into the middle of the square by his hair.

"Now you're going to shut up for good," said the sergeant.

"You can't kill me," said Emilio.

"*¿Que?*"

"If you kill me, I'll be reborn as the people. *Soy el pueblo.* I am the people. You can never kill me. I'll come back and fight, over and over. I live forever, and there's nothing you can do to change that."

THE END.

Please visit www.davidbassano.com for more information about the author.

**More books from
Harvard Square Editions:**

People and Peppers, Kelvin Christopher James
Gates of Eden, Charles Degelman
Love's Affliction, Fidelis Mkparu
Transoceanic Lights, S. Li
Close, Erika Raskin
The Beard, Alan Swyer
Living Treasures, Yang Huang
Nature's Confession, J.L. Morin
Upper West Side Story, Susan Pashman
Dark Lady of Hollywood, Diane Haithman
Fugue for the Right Hand, Michele Tolela Myers
Growing Up White, James P. Stobaugh
Birds of Passage, Joe Giordano
Parallel, Sharon Erby

CPSIA information can be obtained at www.ICGtesting.com
Printed in the USA
BVOW02s1138200916

462717BV00001B/1/P